# My Life Beyond
# VACCINES

A Mayo Clinic patient story
by Hey Gee and Grace Bowden

# Foreword

My favorite genre has always been fantasy, and I especially love dragons. My favorite book series as a kid was *Wings of Fire*, and my favorite movie was *How to Train Your Dragon*. I love how the main character in that movie teaches everyone that dragons aren't so dangerous once people learn to understand the dragons' behavior.

While I was in high school, the COVID-19 pandemic shut down normal life around the world. COVID-19 is caused by a **virus**, and at first, people had no protection against it.

In this story, the main character learns about several new dragons in her kingdom so that she can protect herself and others from them. That's kind of like how scientists study **germs** and develop vaccines for different **germs** that can make you sick. (Even though that may not seem as exciting!)

Now most people can get protection from **vaccines** for COVID-19 and many other diseases. Vaccines are amazing because they can safely teach your immune system to recognize **germs** before you're ever infected with the real thing. Then, if you are exposed to those harmful germs, your body already knows how to fight off an **infection**.

Although **vaccines** might seem scary (like dragons) at first, **vaccines** protect us and help us to grow up healthy and strong. With knowledge and understanding, everyone can help protect themselves and others.

Knowledge is power.

Grace Bowden

"

# KNOWLEDGE IS POWER

"

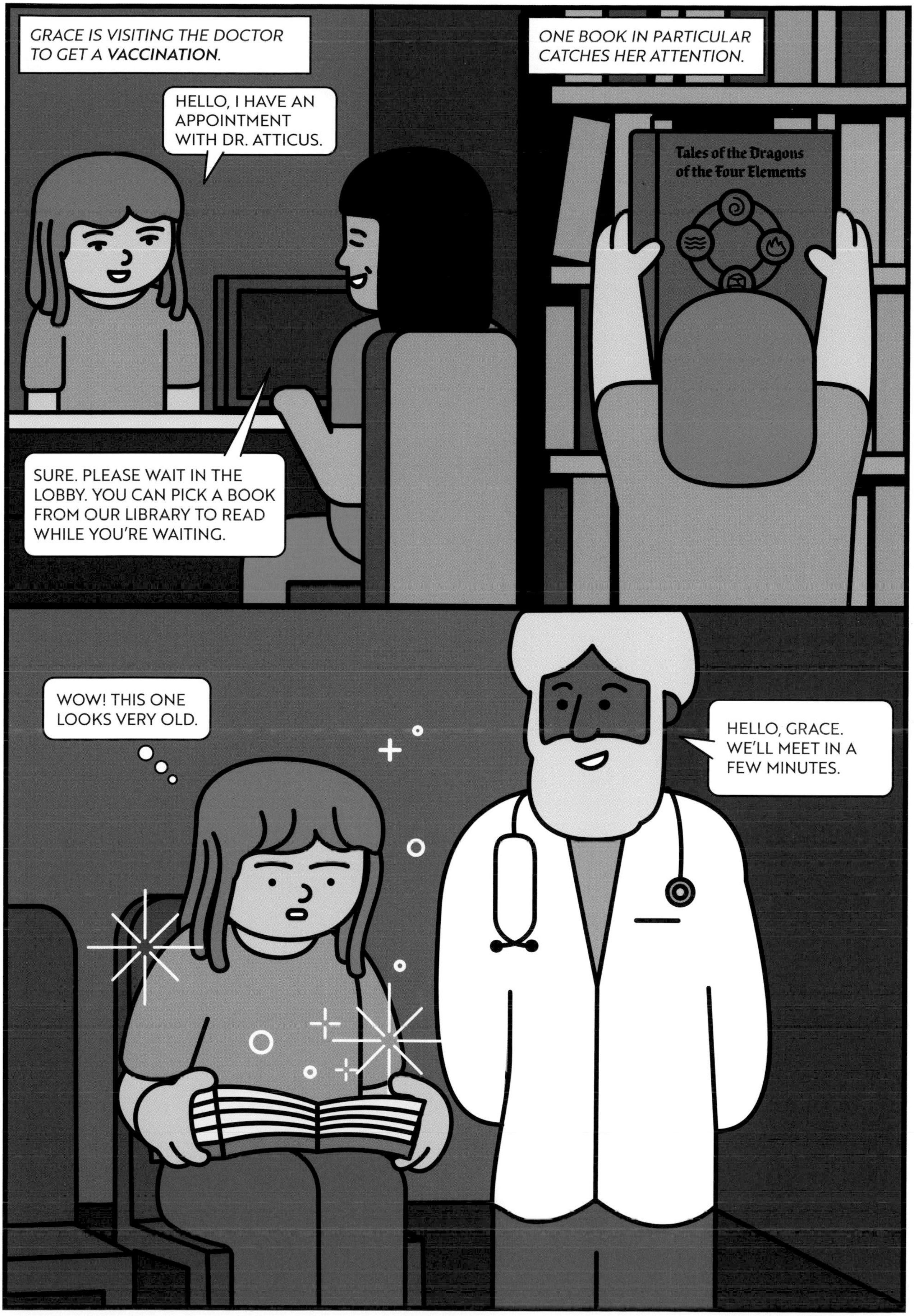
GRACE IS VISITING THE DOCTOR TO GET A VACCINATION.
HELLO, I HAVE AN APPOINTMENT WITH DR. ATTICUS.
SURE. PLEASE WAIT IN THE LOBBY. YOU CAN PICK A BOOK FROM OUR LIBRARY TO READ WHILE YOU'RE WAITING.
ONE BOOK IN PARTICULAR CATCHES HER ATTENTION.
Tales of the Dragons of the Four Elements
WOW! THIS ONE LOOKS VERY OLD.
HELLO, GRACE. WE'LL MEET IN A FEW MINUTES.

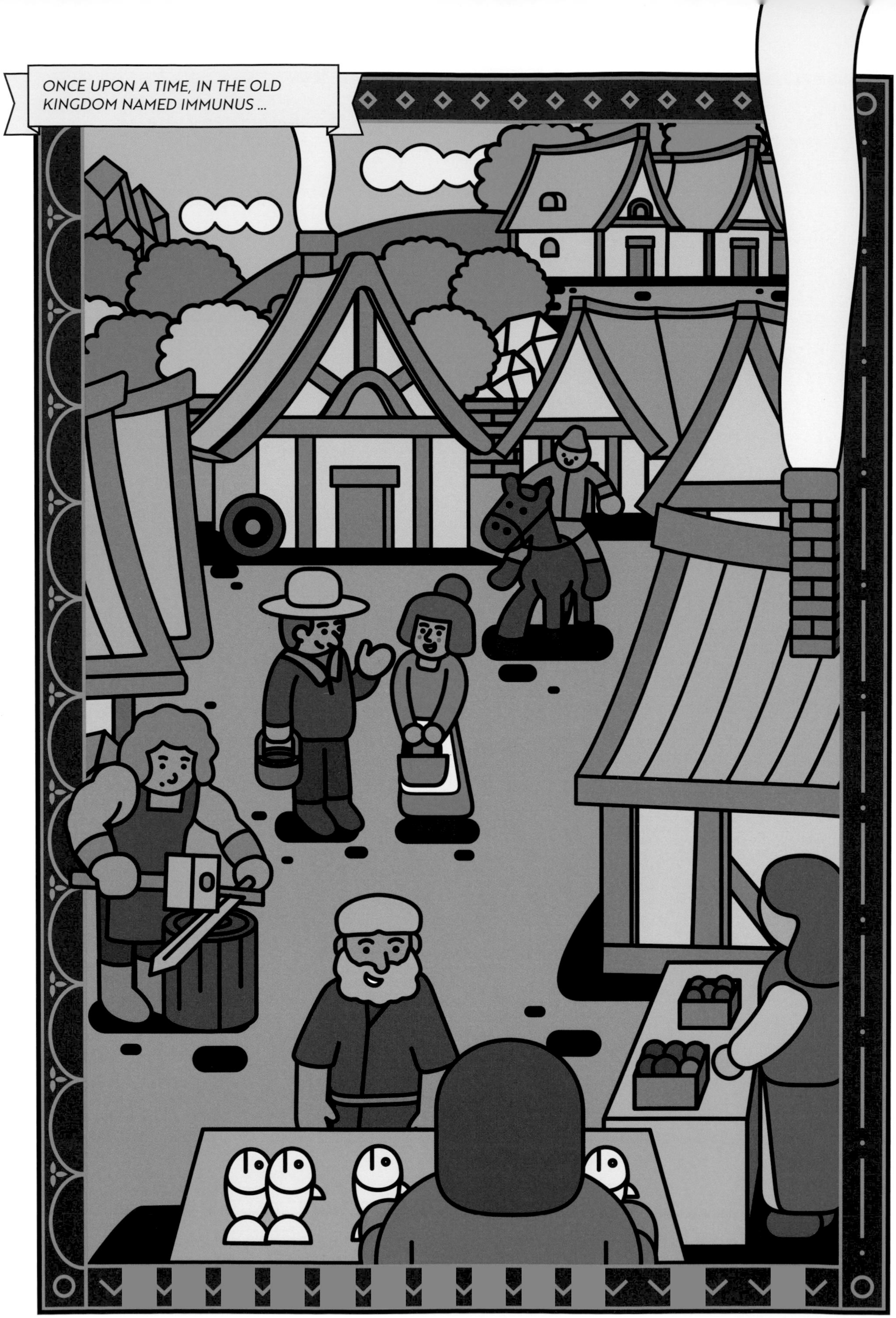
ONCE UPON A TIME, IN THE OLD KINGDOM NAMED IMMUNUS ...

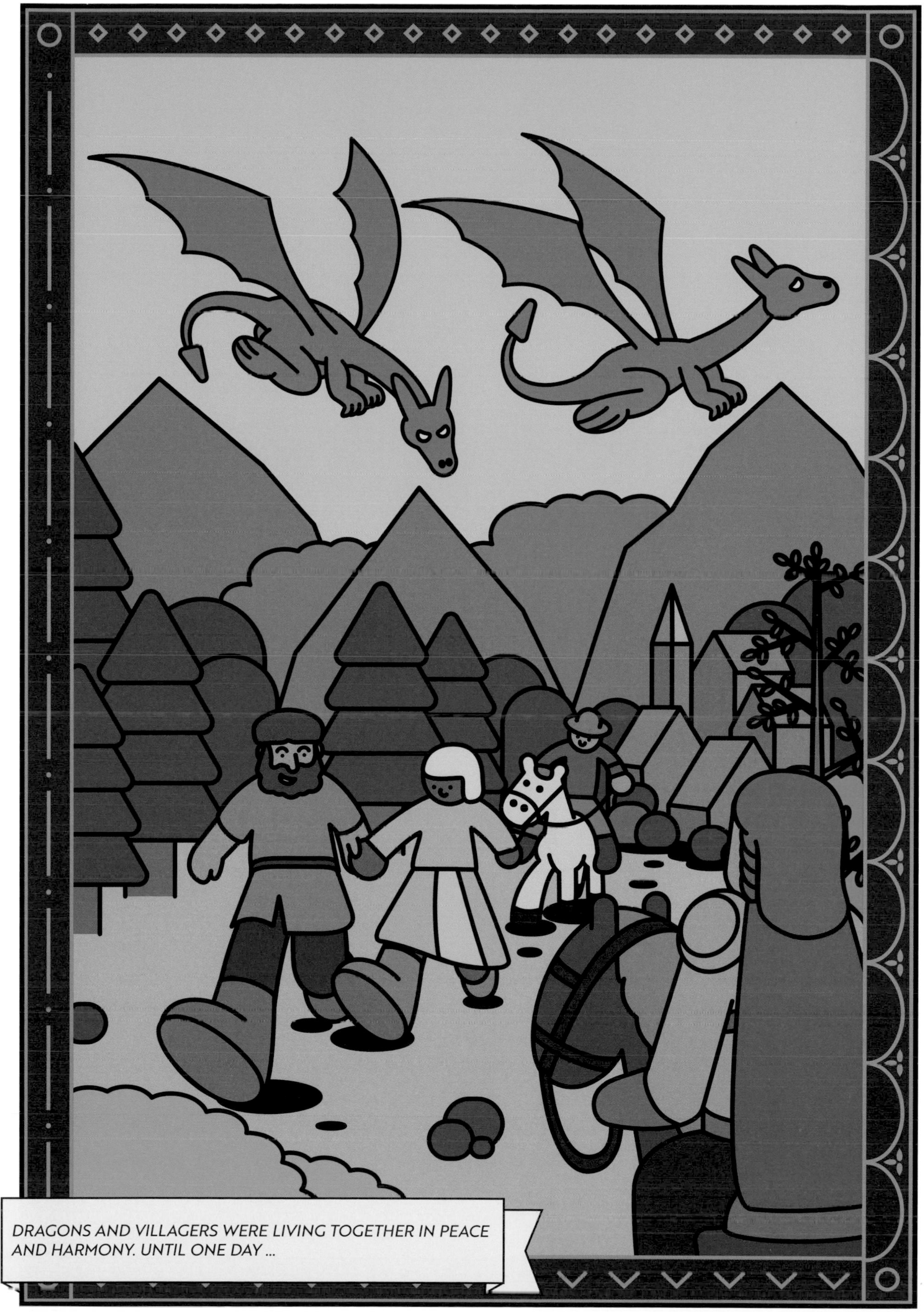
DRAGONS AND VILLAGERS WERE LIVING TOGETHER IN PEACE AND HARMONY. UNTIL ONE DAY ...

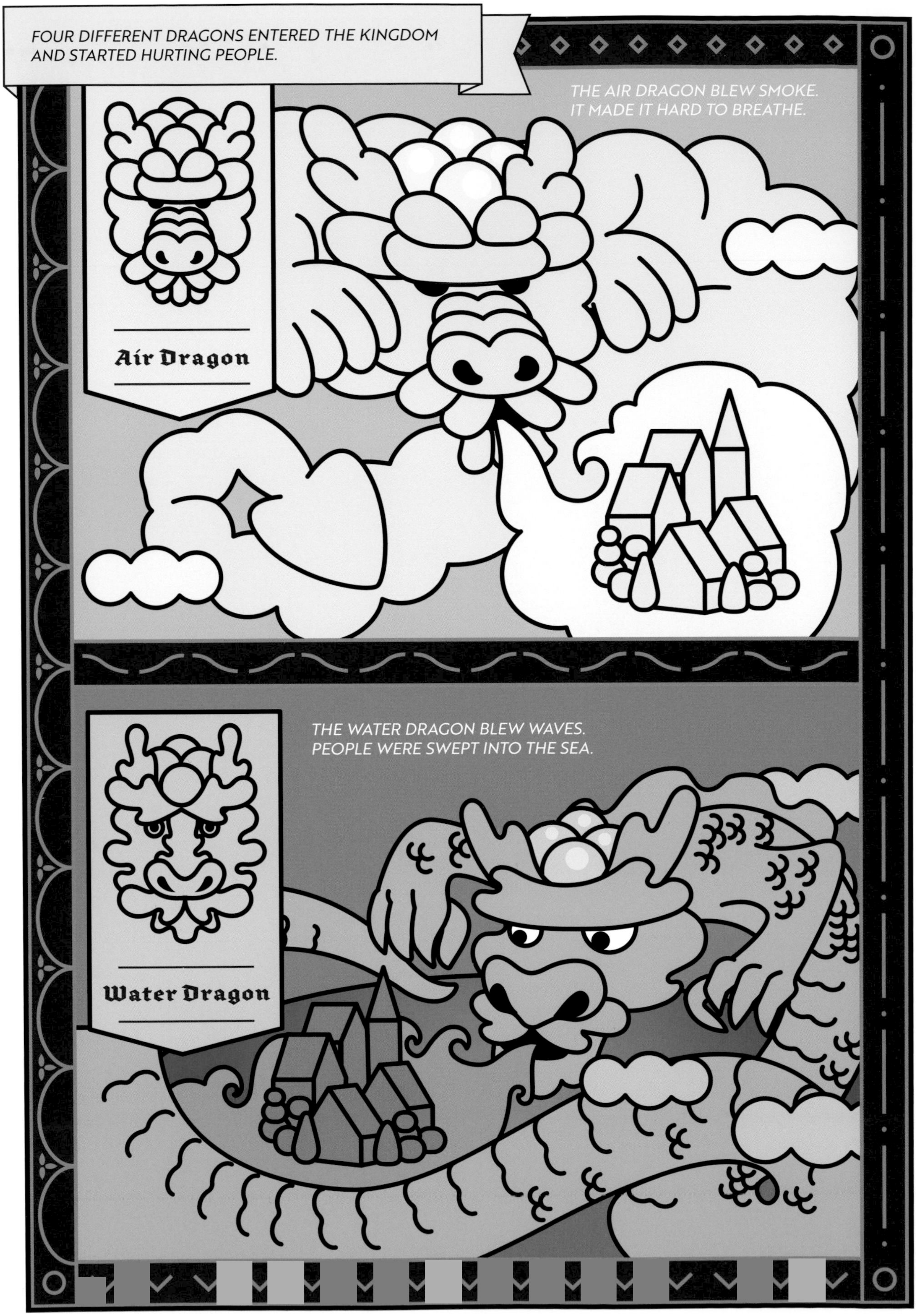
FOUR DIFFERENT DRAGONS ENTERED THE KINGDOM AND STARTED HURTING PEOPLE.
THE AIR DRAGON BLEW SMOKE. IT MADE IT HARD TO BREATHE.
Air Dragon
THE WATER DRAGON BLEW WAVES. PEOPLE WERE SWEPT INTO THE SEA.
Water Dragon

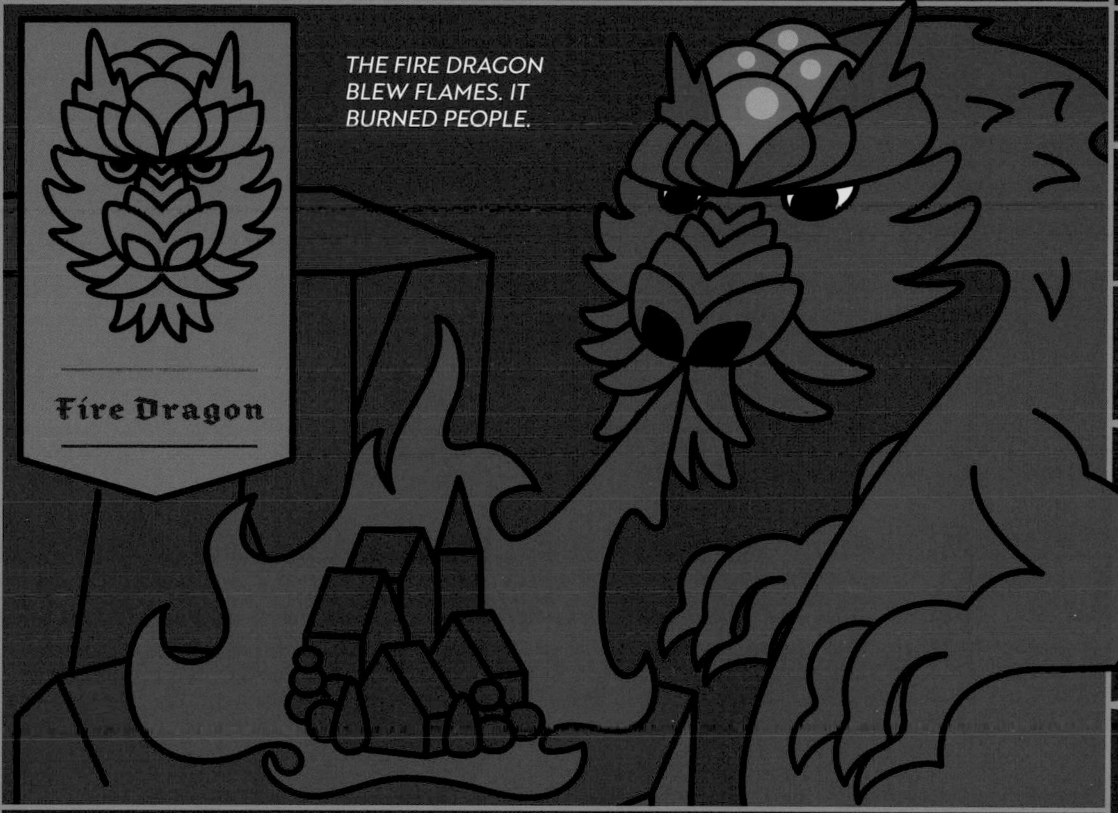
THE FIRE DRAGON BLEW FLAMES. IT BURNED PEOPLE.
Fire Dragon

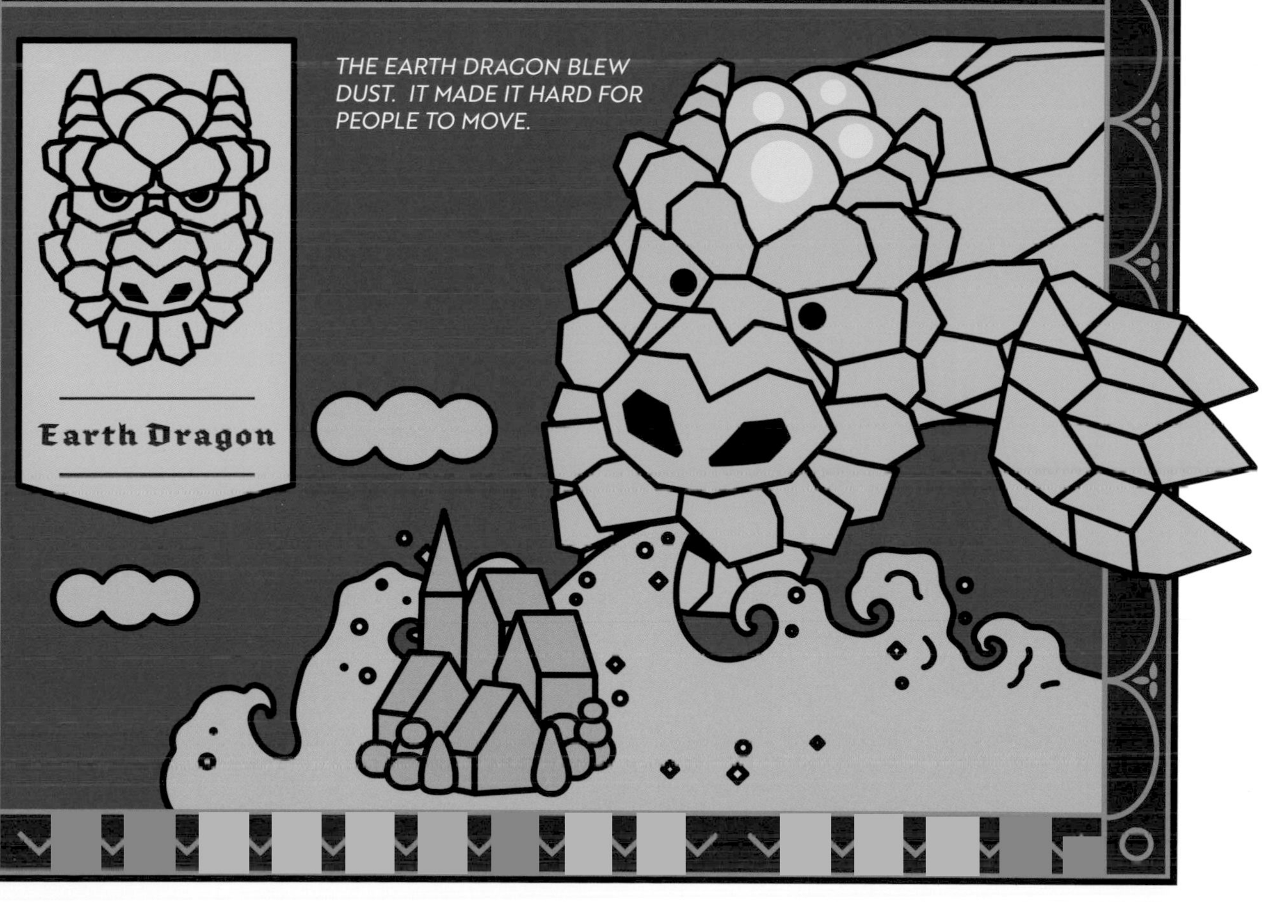
THE EARTH DRAGON BLEW DUST. IT MADE IT HARD FOR PEOPLE TO MOVE.
Earth Dragon

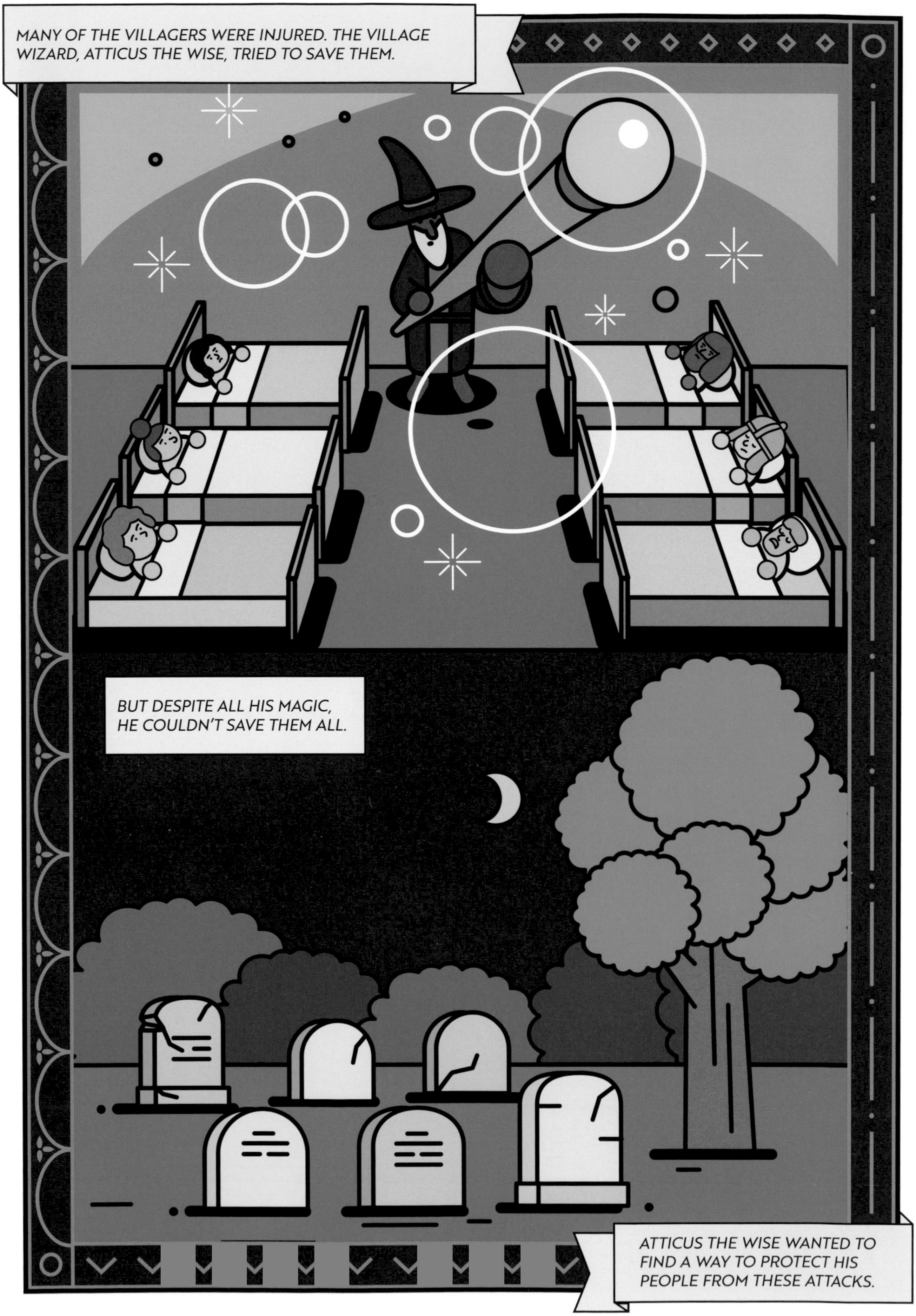
MANY OF THE VILLAGERS WERE INJURED. THE VILLAGE WIZARD, ATTICUS THE WISE, TRIED TO SAVE THEM.
BUT DESPITE ALL HIS MAGIC, HE COULDN'T SAVE THEM ALL.
ATTICUS THE WISE WANTED TO FIND A WAY TO PROTECT HIS PEOPLE FROM THESE ATTACKS.

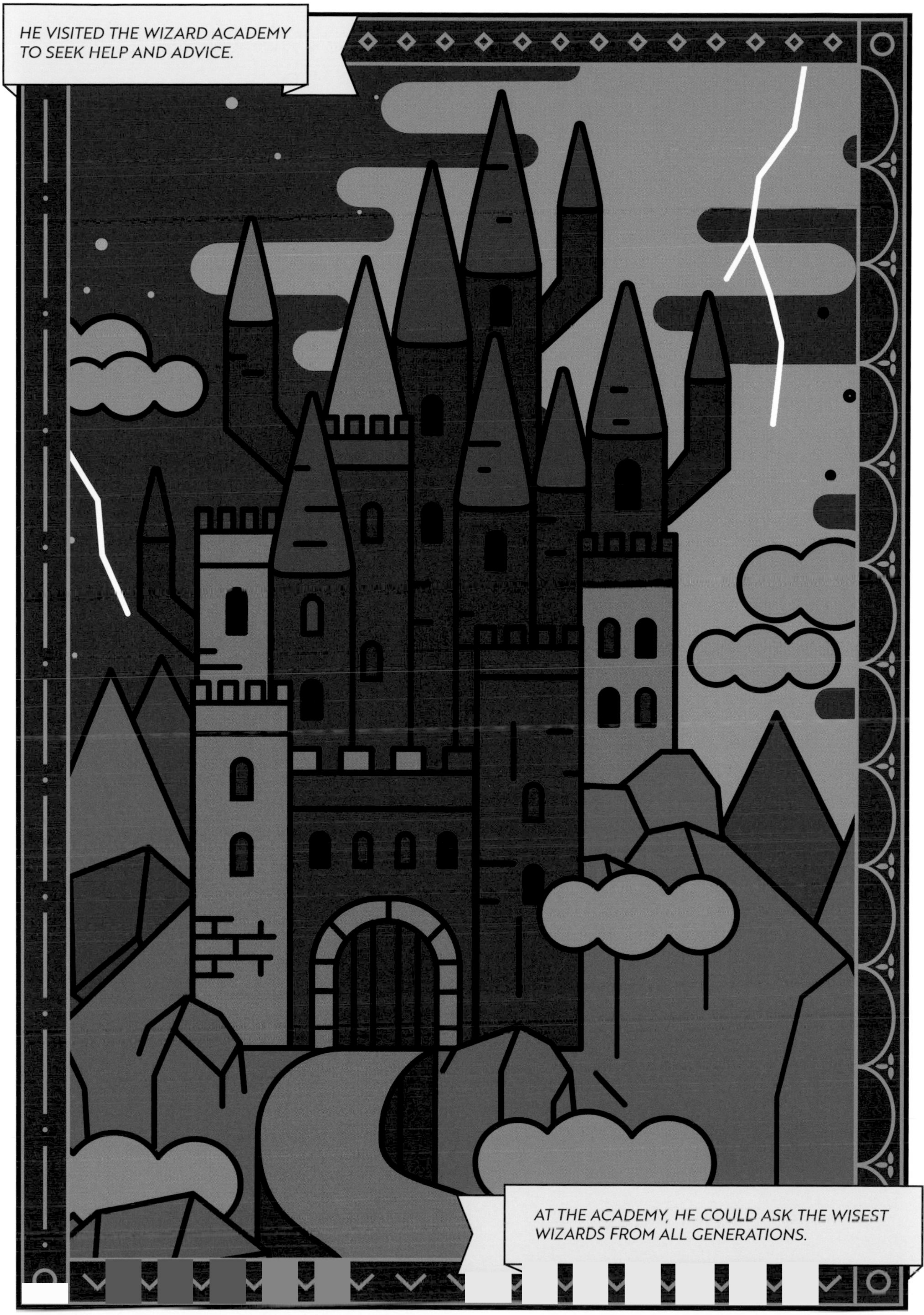
HE VISITED THE WIZARD ACADEMY TO SEEK HELP AND ADVICE.
AT THE ACADEMY, HE COULD ASK THE WISEST WIZARDS FROM ALL GENERATIONS.

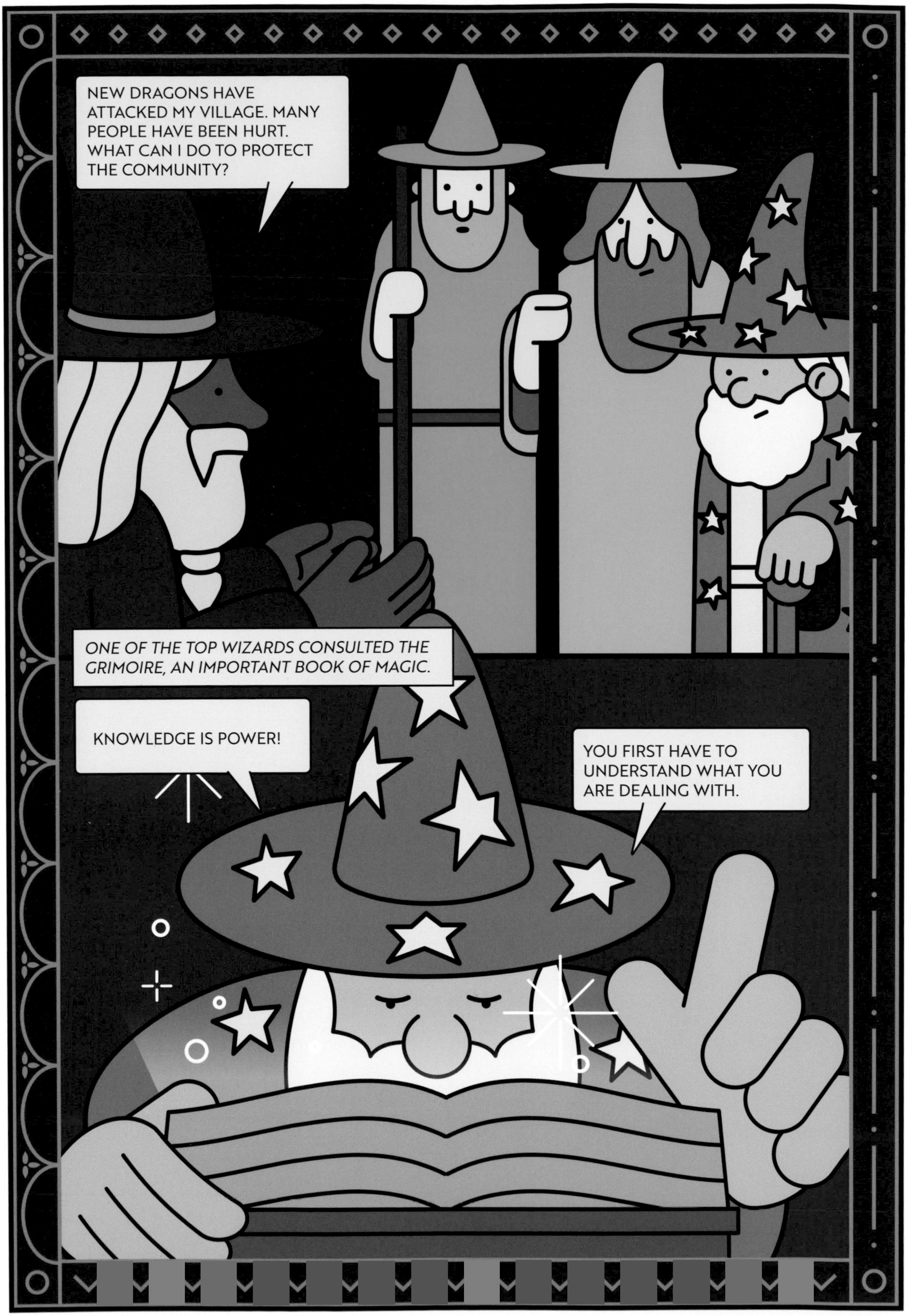
NEW DRAGONS HAVE ATTACKED MY VILLAGE. MANY PEOPLE HAVE BEEN HURT. WHAT CAN I DO TO PROTECT THE COMMUNITY?
*ONE OF THE TOP WIZARDS CONSULTED THE GRIMOIRE, AN IMPORTANT BOOK OF MAGIC.*
KNOWLEDGE IS POWER!
YOU FIRST HAVE TO UNDERSTAND WHAT YOU ARE DEALING WITH.

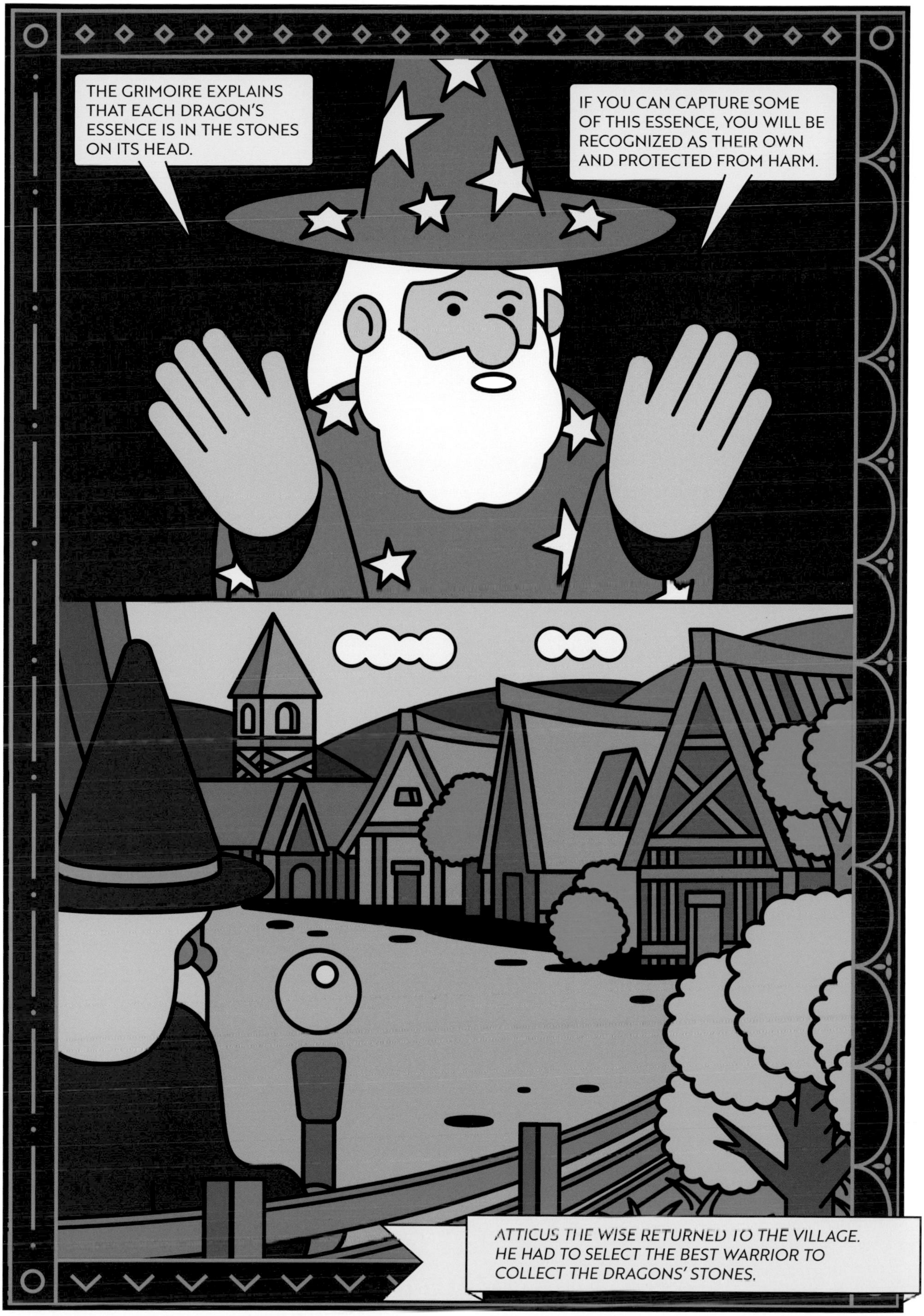
THE GRIMOIRE EXPLAINS THAT EACH DRAGON'S ESSENCE IS IN THE STONES ON ITS HEAD.
IF YOU CAN CAPTURE SOME OF THIS ESSENCE, YOU WILL BE RECOGNIZED AS THEIR OWN AND PROTECTED FROM HARM.
ATTICUS THE WISE RETURNED TO THE VILLAGE. HE HAD TO SELECT THE BEST WARRIOR TO COLLECT THE DRAGONS' STONES.

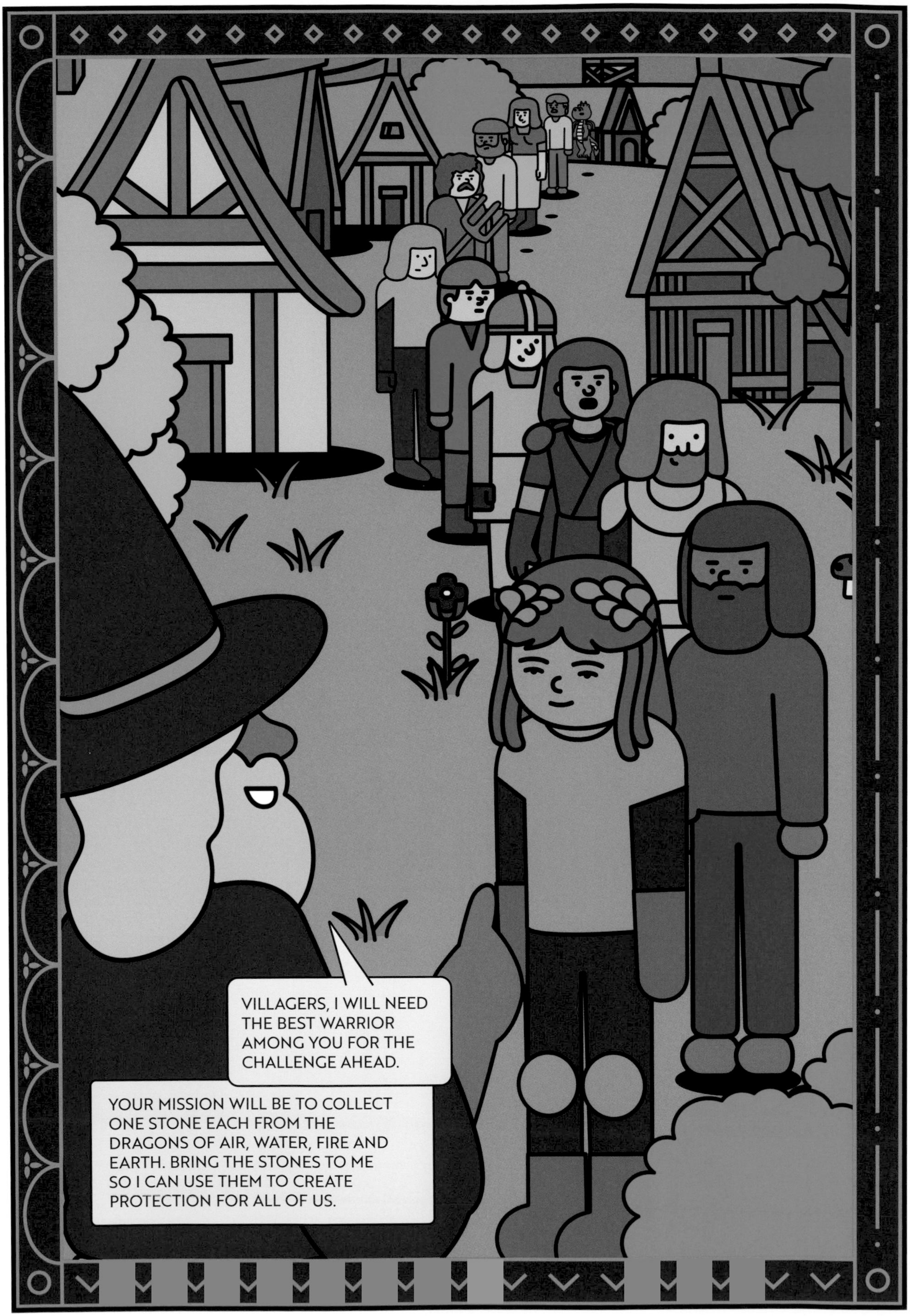
VILLAGERS, I WILL NEED THE BEST WARRIOR AMONG YOU FOR THE CHALLENGE AHEAD.
YOUR MISSION WILL BE TO COLLECT ONE STONE EACH FROM THE DRAGONS OF AIR, WATER, FIRE AND EARTH. BRING THE STONES TO ME SO I CAN USE THEM TO CREATE PROTECTION FOR ALL OF US.

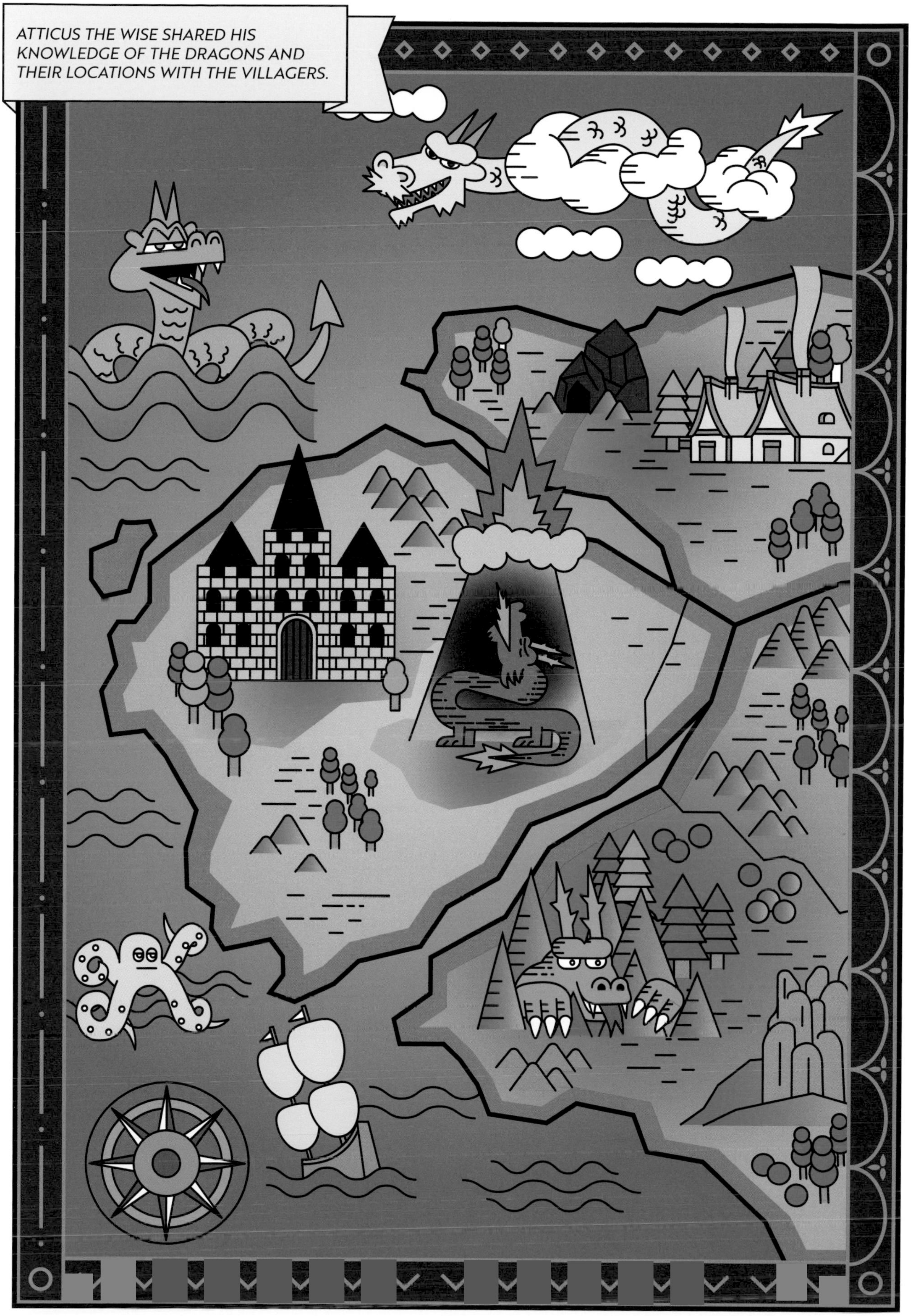
ATTICUS THE WISE SHARED HIS KNOWLEDGE OF THE DRAGONS AND THEIR LOCATIONS WITH THE VILLAGERS.

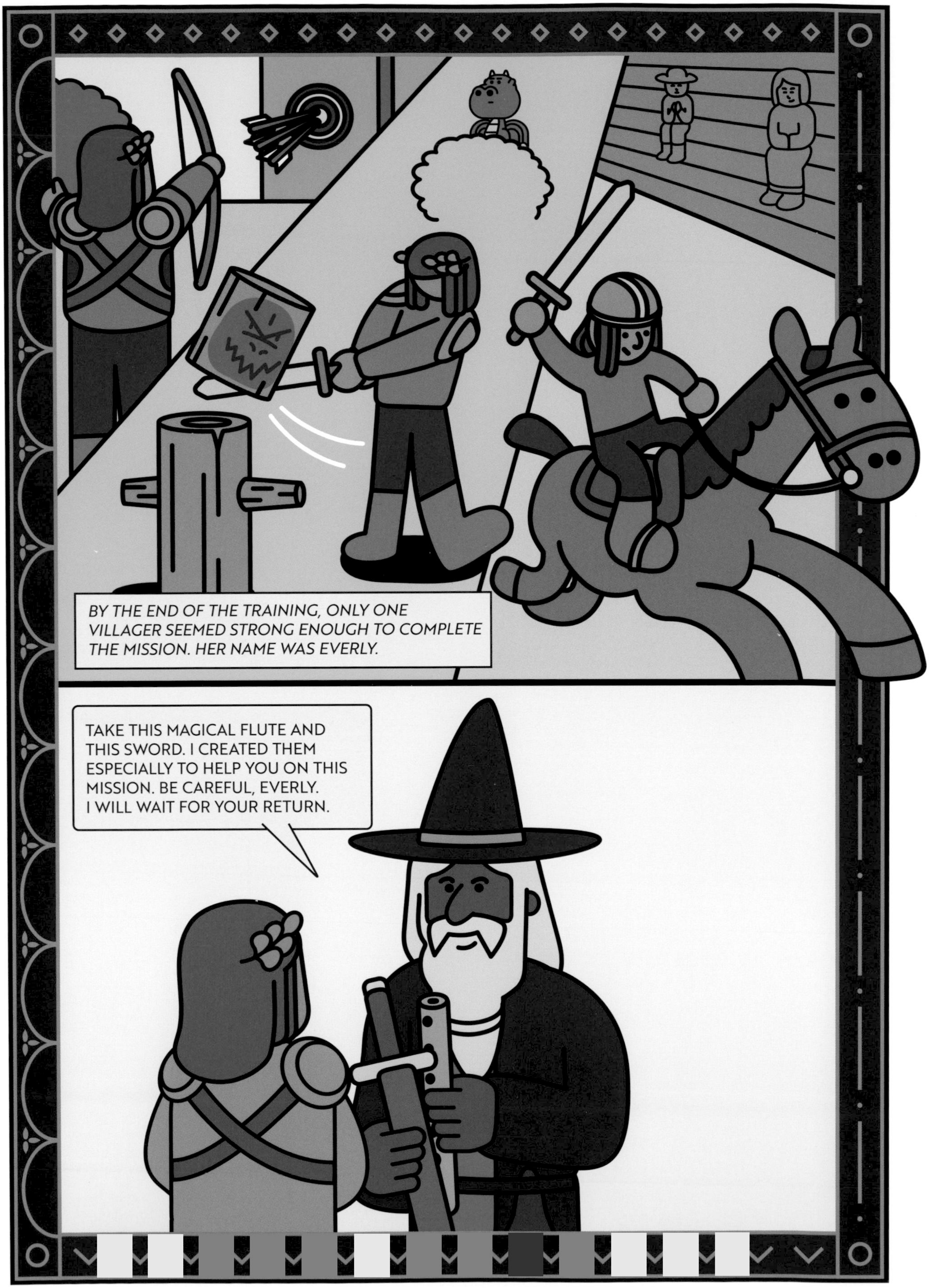
BY THE END OF THE TRAINING, ONLY ONE VILLAGER SEEMED STRONG ENOUGH TO COMPLETE THE MISSION. HER NAME WAS EVERLY.
TAKE THIS MAGICAL FLUTE AND THIS SWORD. I CREATED THEM ESPECIALLY TO HELP YOU ON THIS MISSION. BE CAREFUL, EVERLY. I WILL WAIT FOR YOUR RETURN.

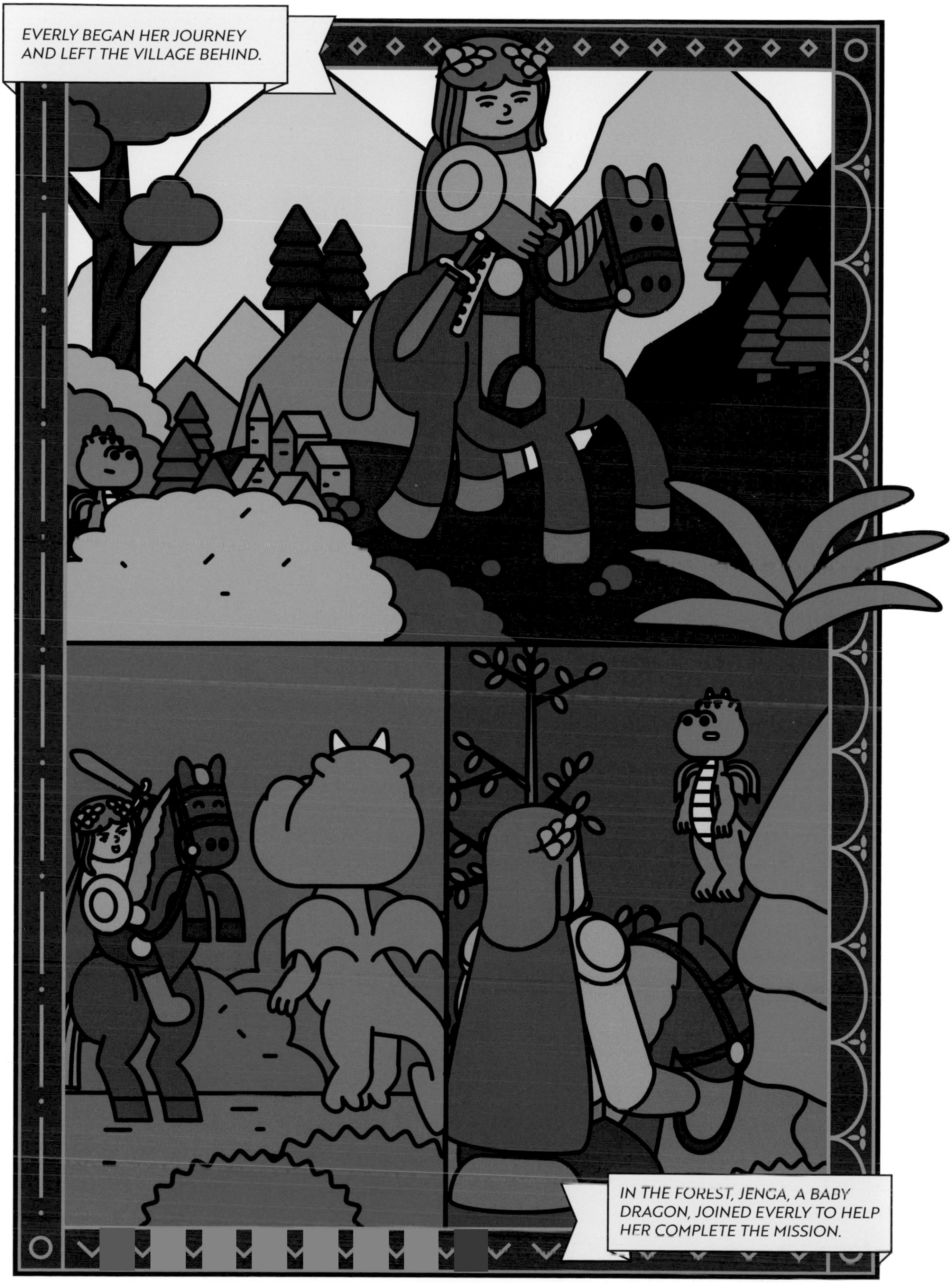
EVERLY BEGAN HER JOURNEY AND LEFT THE VILLAGE BEHIND.
IN THE FOREST, JENGA, A BABY DRAGON, JOINED EVERLY TO HELP HER COMPLETE THE MISSION.

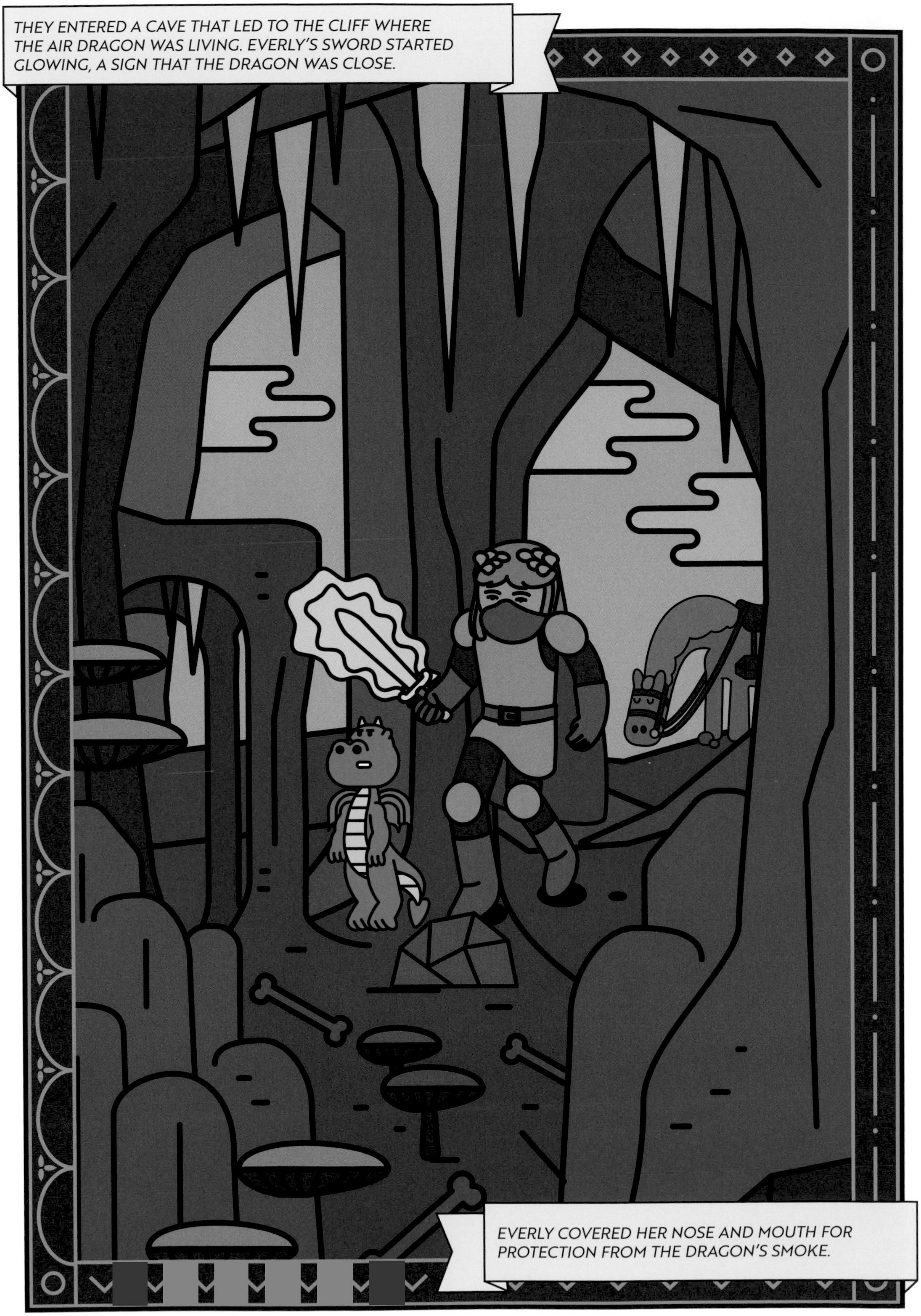
THEY ENTERED A CAVE THAT LED TO THE CLIFF WHERE THE AIR DRAGON WAS LIVING. EVERLY'S SWORD STARTED GLOWING, A SIGN THAT THE DRAGON WAS CLOSE.
EVERLY COVERED HER NOSE AND MOUTH FOR PROTECTION FROM THE DRAGON'S SMOKE.

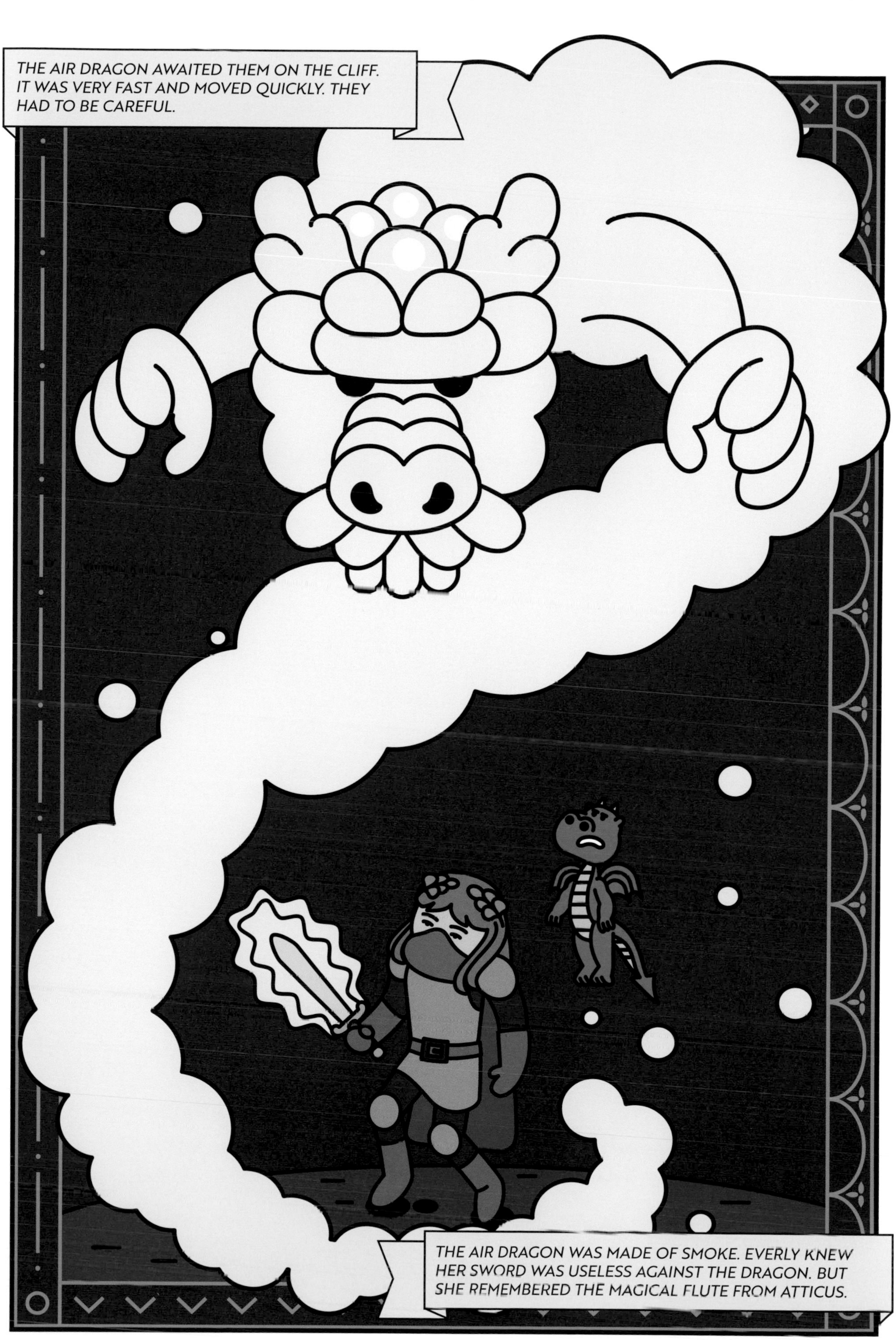
THE AIR DRAGON AWAITED THEM ON THE CLIFF. IT WAS VERY FAST AND MOVED QUICKLY. THEY HAD TO BE CAREFUL.
THE AIR DRAGON WAS MADE OF SMOKE. EVERLY KNEW HER SWORD WAS USELESS AGAINST THE DRAGON. BUT SHE REMEMBERED THE MAGICAL FLUTE FROM ATTICUS.

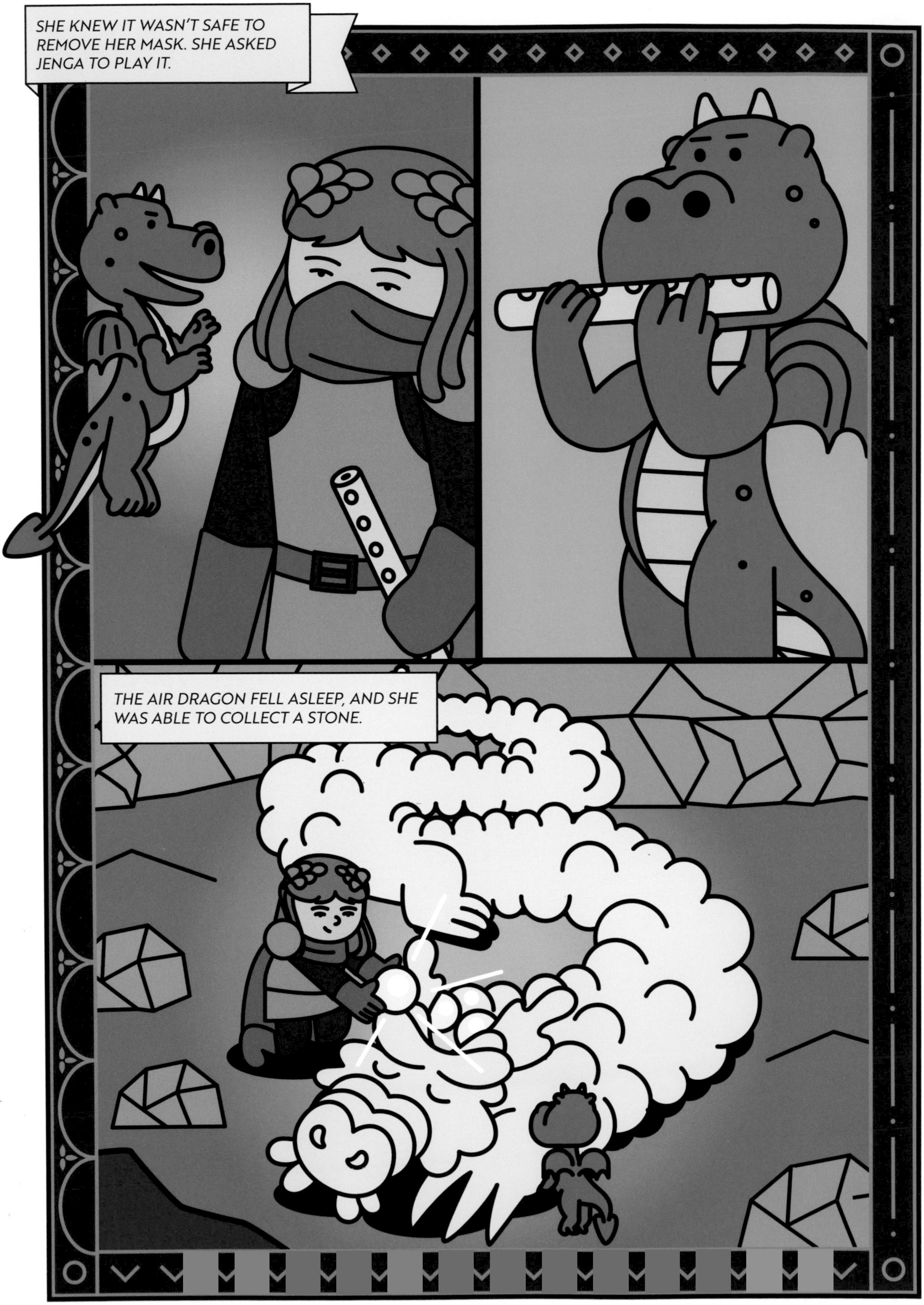
SHE KNEW IT WASN'T SAFE TO REMOVE HER MASK. SHE ASKED JENGA TO PLAY IT.
THE AIR DRAGON FELL ASLEEP, AND SHE WAS ABLE TO COLLECT A STONE.

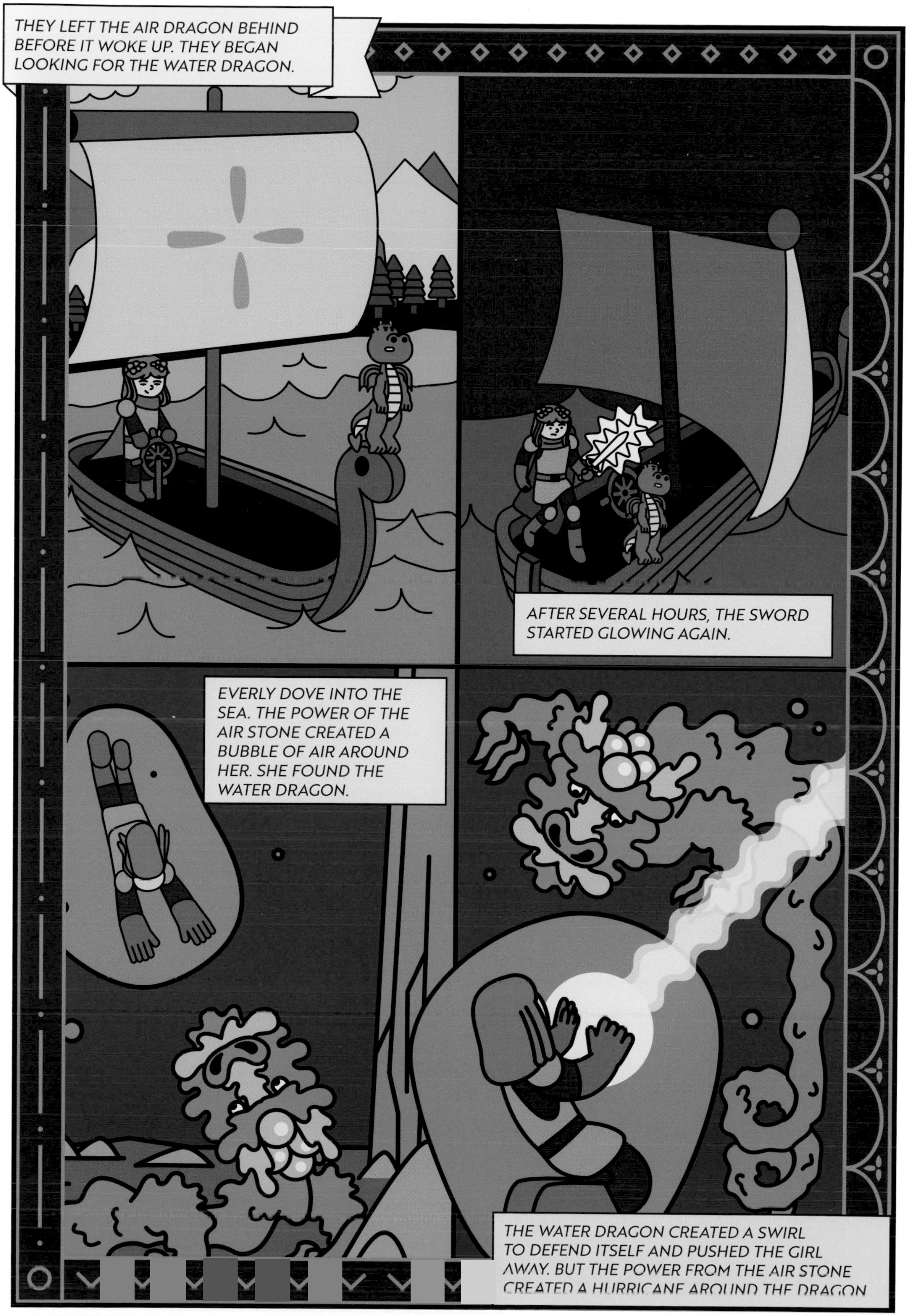
THEY LEFT THE AIR DRAGON BEHIND BEFORE IT WOKE UP. THEY BEGAN LOOKING FOR THE WATER DRAGON.
AFTER SEVERAL HOURS, THE SWORD STARTED GLOWING AGAIN.
EVERLY DOVE INTO THE SEA. THE POWER OF THE AIR STONE CREATED A BUBBLE OF AIR AROUND HER. SHE FOUND THE WATER DRAGON.
THE WATER DRAGON CREATED A SWIRL TO DEFEND ITSELF AND PUSHED THE GIRL AWAY. BUT THE POWER FROM THE AIR STONE CREATED A HURRICANE AROUND THE DRAGON

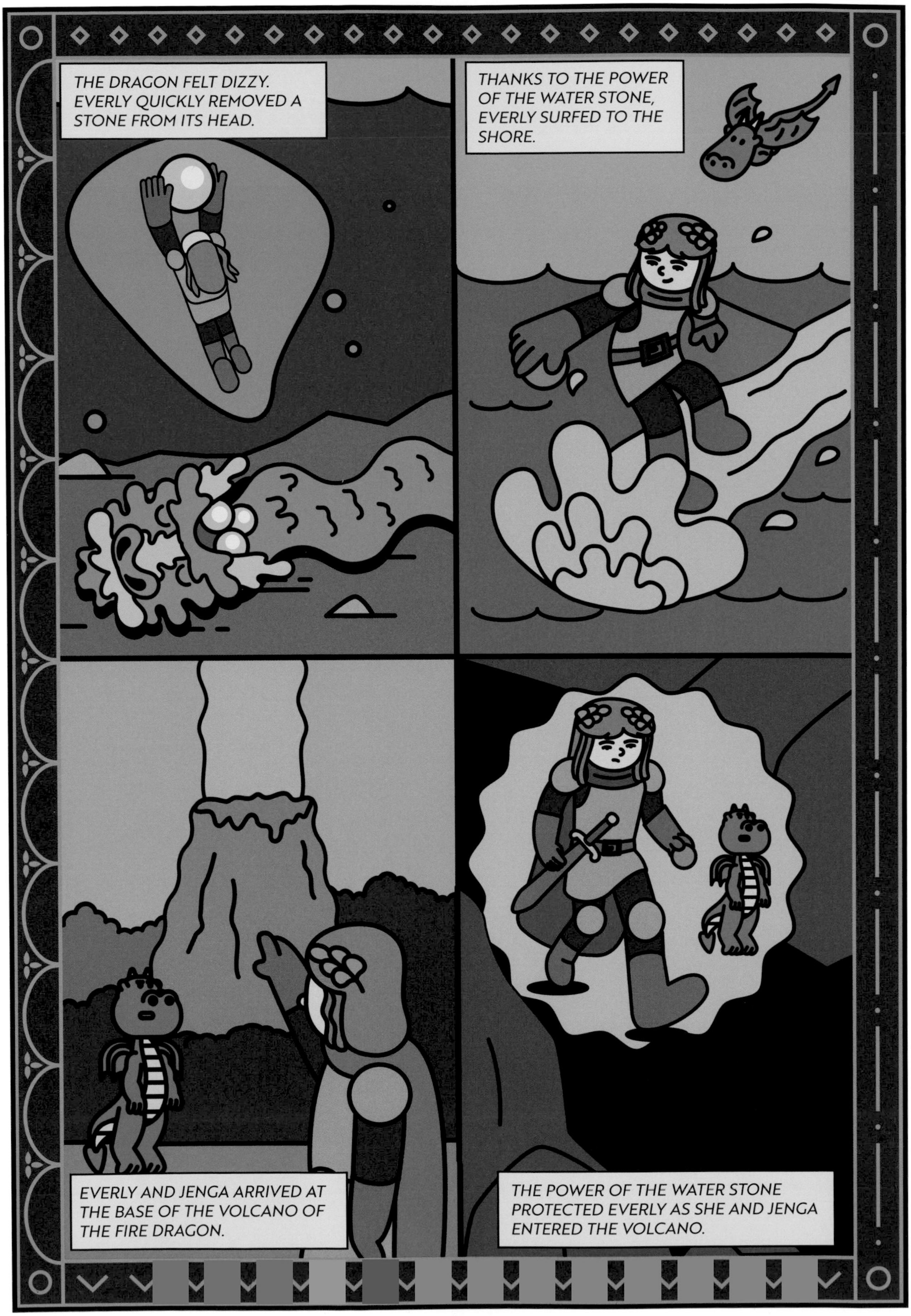
THE DRAGON FELT DIZZY. EVERLY QUICKLY REMOVED A STONE FROM ITS HEAD.
THANKS TO THE POWER OF THE WATER STONE, EVERLY SURFED TO THE SHORE.
EVERLY AND JENGA ARRIVED AT THE BASE OF THE VOLCANO OF THE FIRE DRAGON.
THE POWER OF THE WATER STONE PROTECTED EVERLY AS SHE AND JENGA ENTERED THE VOLCANO.

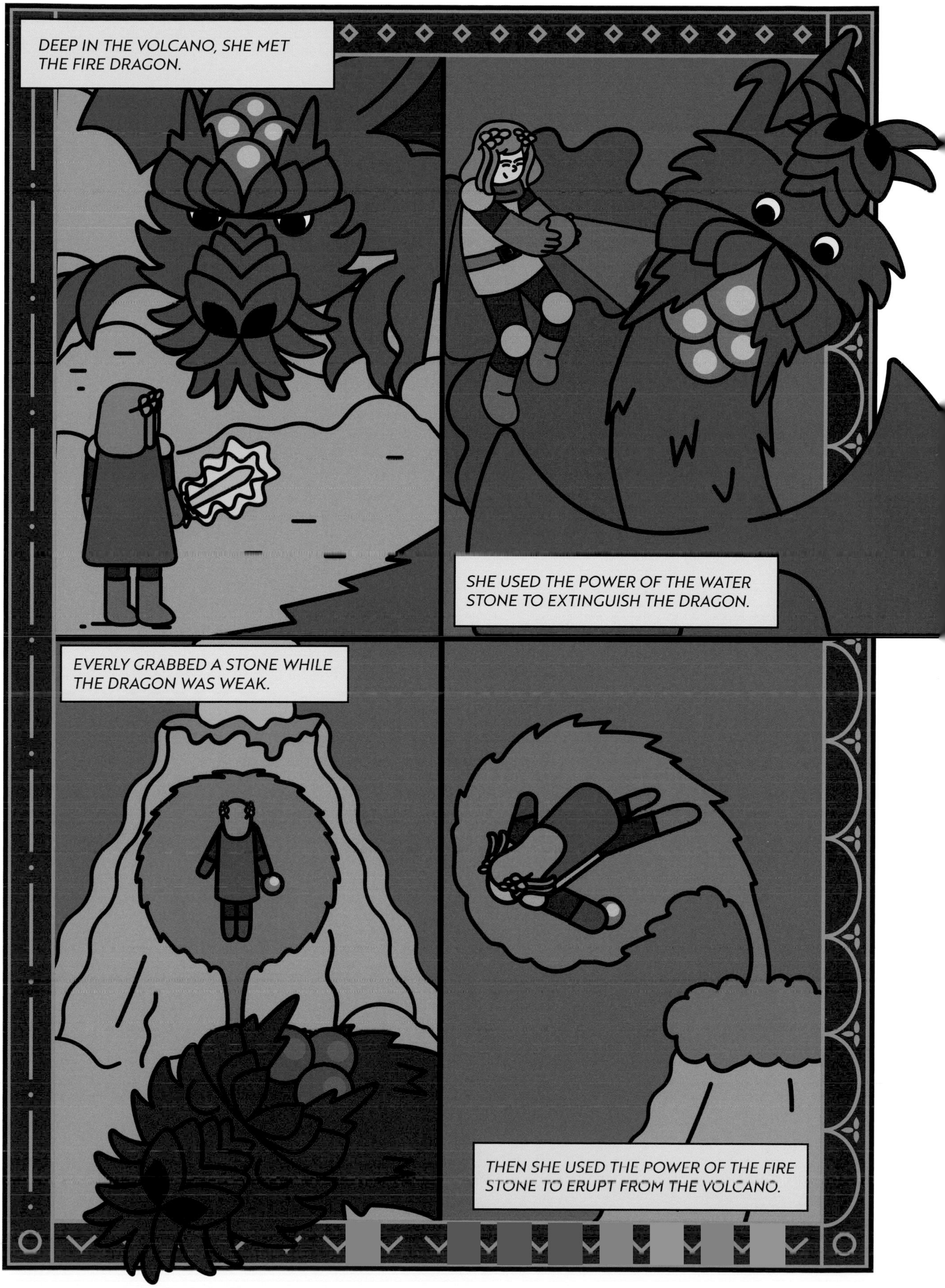
DEEP IN THE VOLCANO, SHE MET THE FIRE DRAGON.
SHE USED THE POWER OF THE WATER STONE TO EXTINGUISH THE DRAGON.
EVERLY GRABBED A STONE WHILE THE DRAGON WAS WEAK.
THEN SHE USED THE POWER OF THE FIRE STONE TO ERUPT FROM THE VOLCANO.

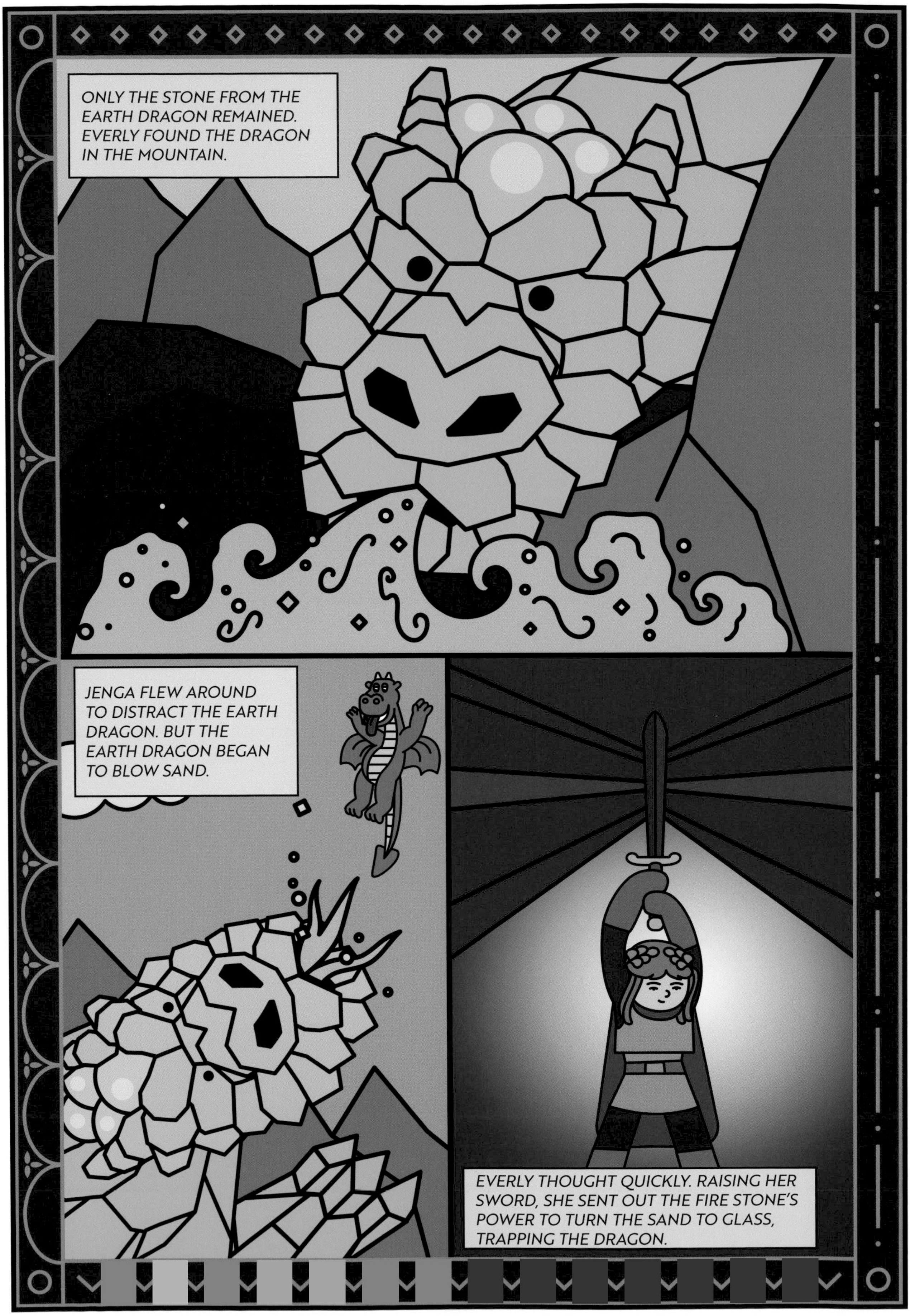
ONLY THE STONE FROM THE EARTH DRAGON REMAINED. EVERLY FOUND THE DRAGON IN THE MOUNTAIN.
JENGA FLEW AROUND TO DISTRACT THE EARTH DRAGON. BUT THE EARTH DRAGON BEGAN TO BLOW SAND.
EVERLY THOUGHT QUICKLY. RAISING HER SWORD, SHE SENT OUT THE FIRE STONE'S POWER TO TURN THE SAND TO GLASS, TRAPPING THE DRAGON.

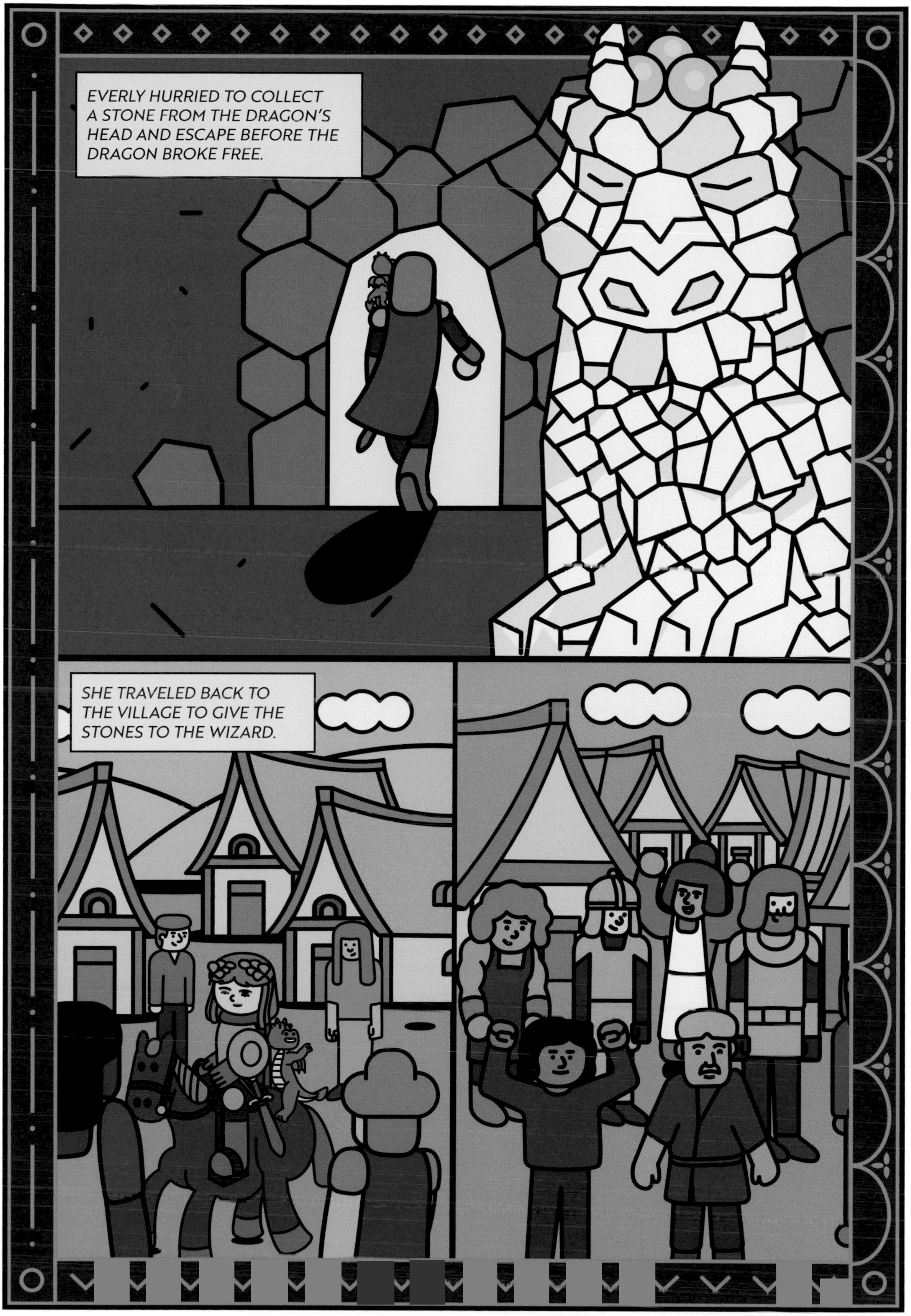
EVERLY HURRIED TO COLLECT A STONE FROM THE DRAGON'S HEAD AND ESCAPE BEFORE THE DRAGON BROKE FREE.
SHE TRAVELED BACK TO THE VILLAGE TO GIVE THE STONES TO THE WIZARD.

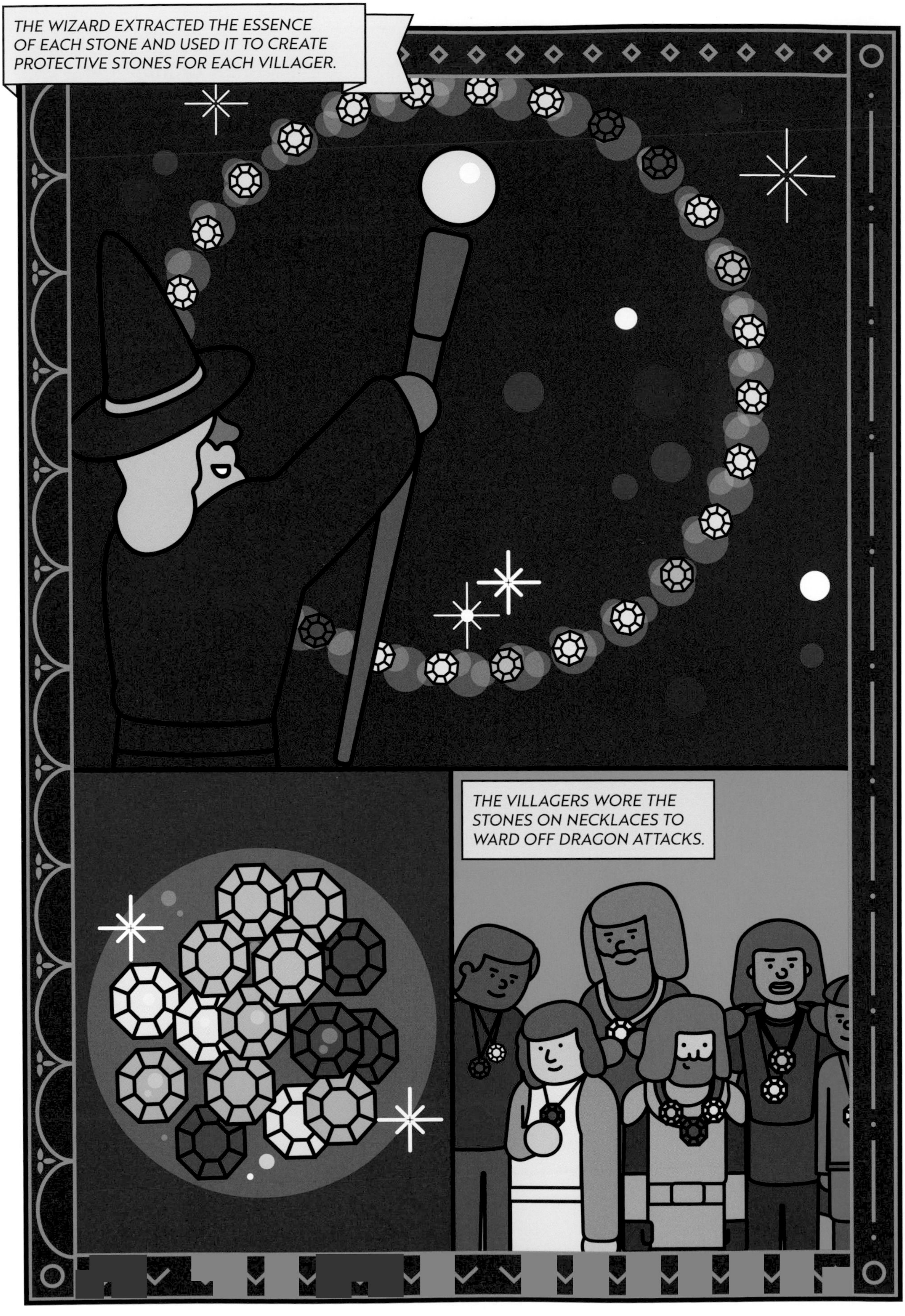
THE WIZARD EXTRACTED THE ESSENCE OF EACH STONE AND USED IT TO CREATE PROTECTIVE STONES FOR EACH VILLAGER.
THE VILLAGERS WORE THE STONES ON NECKLACES TO WARD OFF DRAGON ATTACKS.

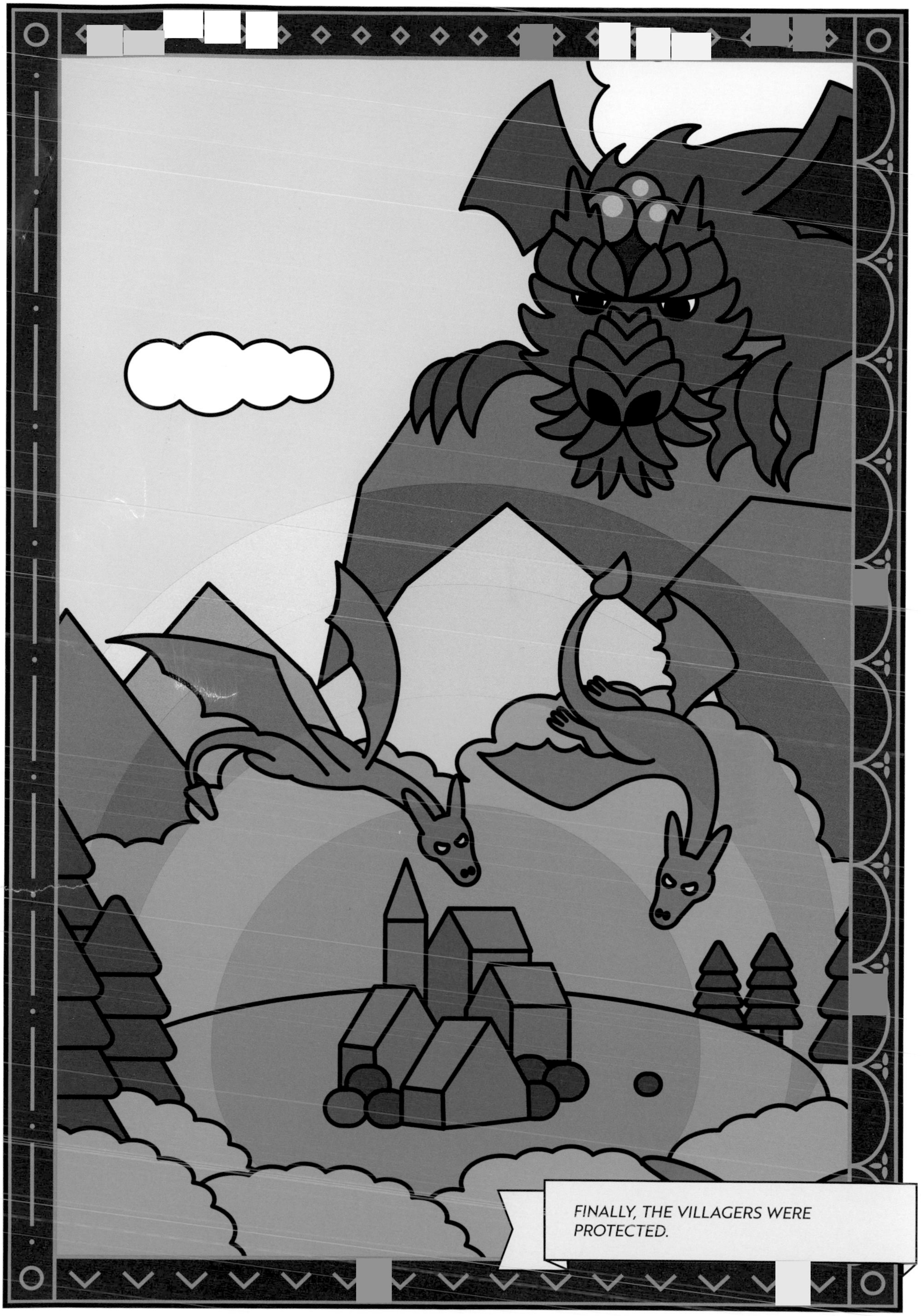
FINALLY, THE VILLAGERS WERE PROTECTED.

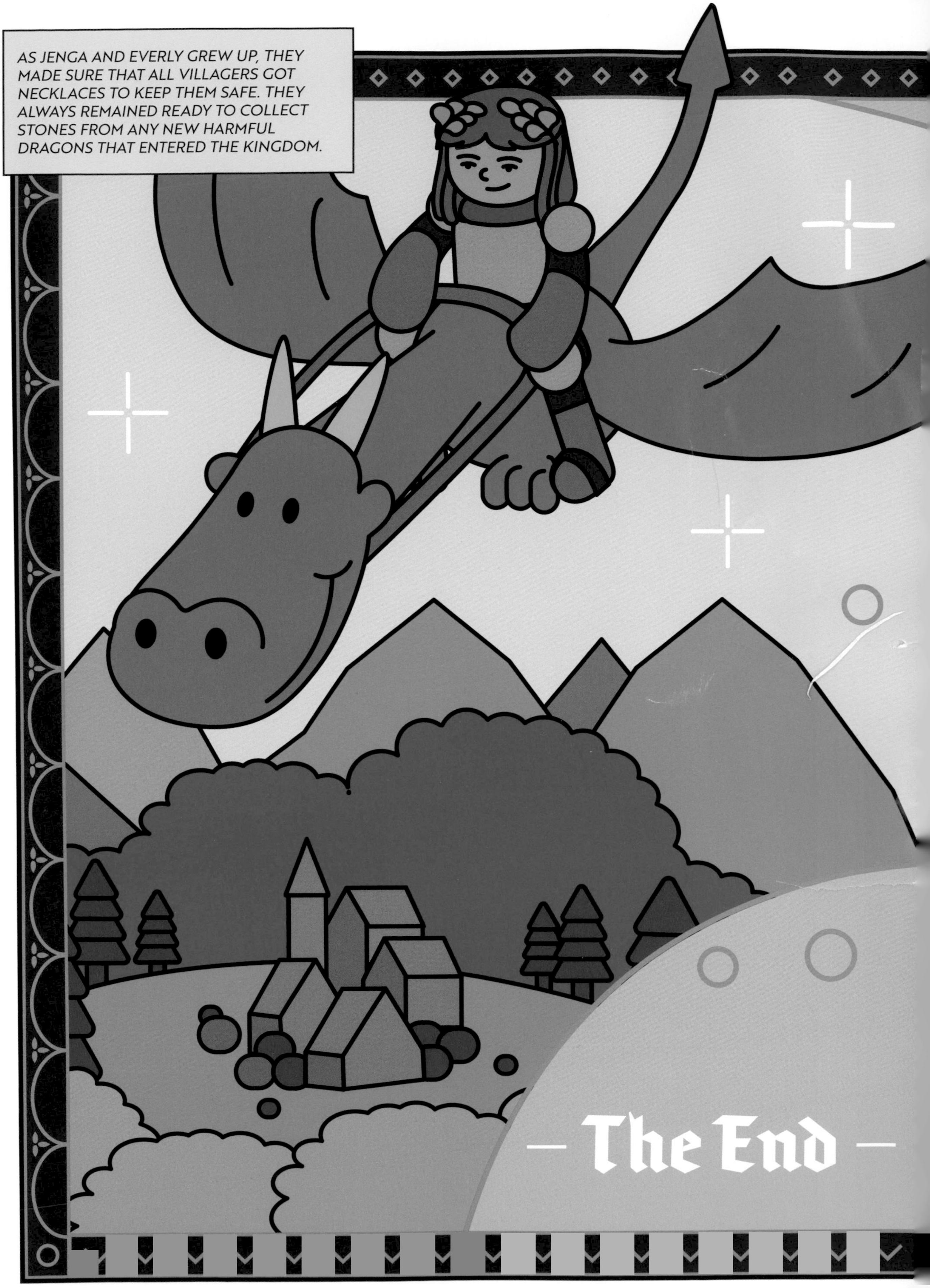
AS JENGA AND EVERLY GREW UP, THEY MADE SURE THAT ALL VILLAGERS GOT NECKLACES TO KEEP THEM SAFE. THEY ALWAYS REMAINED READY TO COLLECT STONES FROM ANY NEW HARMFUL DRAGONS THAT ENTERED THE KINGDOM.
— The End —

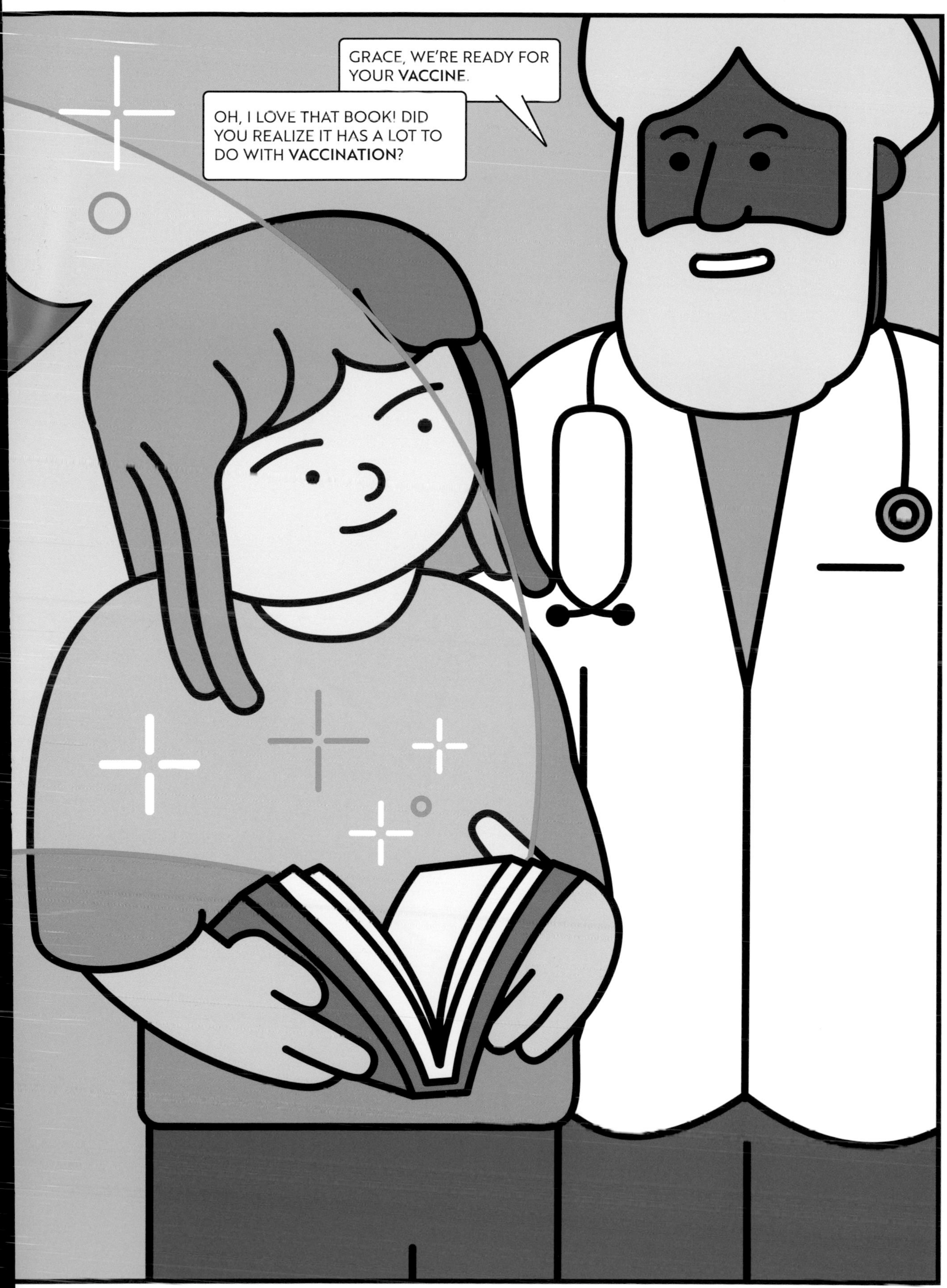
GRACE, WE'RE READY FOR YOUR VACCINE.
OH, I LOVE THAT BOOK! DID YOU REALIZE IT HAS A LOT TO DO WITH VACCINATION?

## KEY TERMS

**bacteria**: tiny, one-celled living organisms that breathe and eat. They live and grow and can make more bacteria. Some are harmless, while others are germs that can make people sick.

**germs**: bacteria, viruses, fungi and other microbes that can cause infection. Germs live everywhere. They cause infection and disease by getting around the defenses of your immune system.

**immunity**: protection from infection that you get when your immune system learns to fight certain germs. This protection might be long term or only short term. You can develop immunity after an infection or by getting a vaccine.

**immunization**: a process or a type of medicine that gives people short-term or long-term protection from certain infections

**infection**: illness caused by a germ

**vaccine**: a type of immunization that teaches the body to make long-term protection from certain germs

**viruses**: near-living germs that are tiny capsules of genetic material. The genetic material is the code the body needs to make more viruses. Viruses don't breathe or eat. They hijack cells in your body to reproduce.

## MORE INFORMATION FROM THE MEDICAL EDITOR

**by Robert M. Jacobson, M.D.**
**Division of Community Pediatric and Adolescent Medicine, Department of Pediatric and Adolescent Medicine, Children's Center, Mayo Clinic, Rochester, MN**

**Vaccines** are among the safest treatments that doctors can give their patients, with the greatest payoff. That's because they help protect people from **germs** that can make them sick.

**Germs** such as **viruses** and **bacteria** live everywhere. **Infections** develop when certain **germs** get into your body and spread. When this happens, your immune system works to stop the infection. It makes antibodies that work against the **germs**. But it can take time for your immune system to make antibodies to fight new **germs**.

Meanwhile, you might feel sick from the infection and your body's response. For example, a measles infection typically causes fever, rash and other symptoms. It can also cause pneumonia or other severe illness.

**Vaccines** give you protection, called active **immunity**, from **infections** and illness. They teach your body to make antibodies and other defenses to fight certain **germs**. Different **vaccines** train your immune system to fight the **viruses** or **bacteria** that cause diseases such as measles, chicken pox, stomach flu (rotavirus) and COVID-19. Then your body can respond quickly next time it meets one of these **germs**.

Vaccines can help prevent many types of illness. When you avoid getting sick, you don't have to miss sports, activities, school and more. Vaccines can even help protect you from serious diseases when you're older. The HPV vaccine, for example, is recommended for 11- and 12-year-olds, and it can help prevent an infection that may lead to cancer in adults. Some vaccines, such as the flu vaccine, may not fully prevent you from getting sick. But they will help protect you from serious illness if you do get infected.

There are several types of vaccines. All can give you long-lasting protection, but they work differently. Some vaccines are live vaccines, which use a weakened form of a germ. The vaccine trains your body to fight off the germ, but it won't make you sick. Often, you need only one or two doses of live vaccines to be protected for life. Other vaccines may be inactivated germs, messenger RNA, proteins or sugar chains. Usually, you'll need several doses of these vaccines to get fully protected. And you'll need booster doses to stay protected.

Research has shown that vaccines are very safe – especially compared to the risks of infections. (Or dragons!) Getting routine vaccines is one of the easiest ways you can stay healthy and protected from the germs you encounter every day.

## REFERENCES

Dudley MZ, et al. The state of vaccine safety science: systematic reviews of the evidence. *The Lancet Infectious Diseases*. 2020; doi:10.1016/S1473-3099(20)30130-4.

Bernstein HH, et al. The need to optimize adolescent immunization. *Pediatrics*. 2017; doi: 10.1542/peds.2016-4186.

## WEB RESOURCES

**HealthyChildren.org – Immunizations — www.healthychildren.org/English/safety-prevention/immunizations/**
Find the most up-to-date immunization schedules on this page from the American Academy of Pediatricians.

**Immunize (formerly Immunization Action Coalition – IAC) — www.immunize.org**
IAC works to improve the immunization rates and prevent diseases. It provides educational material to the public and health professionals. It also facilitates communication about immunization within a community of patients, parents, healthcare organizations and government health agencies.

**Vaccinate your Family — vaccinateyourfamily.org**
This organization aims to protect people from vaccine-preventable diseases by raising awareness of recommended vaccination schedules for children and adults. It works toward a better understanding of the benefits of vaccines and ensuring that everybody has access to lifesaving vaccines.

**Voices for Vaccines — www.voicesforvaccines.org**
This organization develops volunteer networks to publicly communicate accurate information and credible facts about vaccination.

## ABOUT THE MEDICAL EDITOR

**Robert M. Jacobson, M.D.**
**Community Pediatric and Adolescent Medicine, Pediatric and Adolescent Medicine, Children's Center, Mayo Clinic, Rochester, MN**

Robert M. Jacobson, M.D. is a pediatrician at Mayo Clinic in Rochester, Minnesota. He also teaches and researches in the Mayo Clinic College of Medicine and Science, and he serves as a consultant in children's infectious diseases and clinical epidemiology – the study of the spread and causes of diseases. He has special expertise with **vaccines** for people of all ages. Dr. Jacobson directs the Population Health Science Scholars Program at the Kern Center, and he also serves as the medical director for the **immunization** program for Primary Care in Southeast Minnesota. His research on practical ways to improve vaccination rates is supported by the National Institutes of Health.

## ABOUT THE AUTHORS

Guillaume Federighi, aka **Hey Gee**, is a French and American author and illustrator. He began his career in 1998 in Paris, France. He also spent a few decades exploring the world of street art and graffiti in different European capitals. After moving to New York in 2008, he worked with many companies and brands, developing a reputation in graphic design and illustration for his distinctive style of translating complex ideas into simple and timeless visual stories.
He is also the owner and creative director of Hey Gee Studio, a full-service creative agency based in New York City.

**Grace Bowden** learned about human papillomavirus (HPV) during a ninth grade science project. She learned that HPV causes an infection that can lead to certain types of cancer. Anyone can get an HPV infection, but the **vaccine** to prevent it is safe. Grace learned how important **vaccines** are in protecting against HPV and many other infections. Then the COVID-19 pandemic, caused by a **virus**, began when Grace was in 10th grade. Once **vaccines** were available, she wanted to use her voice to help people protect themselves by learning about **vaccines**. Grace is creative and high-spirited, and she loves swimming. She also plays three instruments, sings in choir and has a passion for writing. She wants to thank her mother for inspiring her to learn about **vaccines**, and also Dr. Jacobson and Mayo Clinic for the opportunity to help write this book.

## ABOUT FONDATION IPSEN BOOKLAB

Fondation Ipsen improves the lives of millions of people around the world by rethinking scientific communication. The truthful transmission of science to the public is complex because scientific information is often technical and there is a lot of inaccurate information. In 2018, Fondation Ipsen established BookLab to address this need. BookLab books come about through collaboration between scientists, doctors, artists, authors, and children. In paper and electronic formats, and in several languages, BookLab delivers books across more than 50 countries for people of all ages and cultures. Fondation Ipsen BookLab's publications are free of charge to schools, libraries and people living in precarious situations. Join us! Access and share our books by visiting: www.fondation-ipsen.org.

## ABOUT MAYO CLINIC PRESS

Launched in 2019, Mayo Clinic Press shines a light on the most fascinating stories in medicine and empowers individuals with the knowledge to build healthier, happier lives. From the award-winning Mayo Clinic Health Letter to books and media covering the scope of human health and wellness, Mayo Clinic Press publications provide readers with reliable and trusted content by some of the world's leading health care professionals. Proceeds benefit important medical research and education at Mayo Clinic. For more information about Mayo Clinic Press, visit MCPress.MayoClinic.org.

## ABOUT THE COLLABORATION

The My Life Beyond series was developed in partnership between Fondation Ipsen's BookLab and Mayo Clinic, which has provided world-class medical education for more than 150 years. This collaboration aims to provide trustworthy, impactful resources for understanding childhood diseases and other problems that can affect children's well-being.

The series offers readers a holistic perspective of children's lives with — and beyond — their medical challenges. In creating these books, young people who have been Mayo Clinic patients worked together with author-illustrator Hey Gee, sharing their personal experiences. The resulting fictionalized stories authentically bring to life the patients' emotions and their inspiring responses to challenging circumstances. In addition, Mayo Clinic physicians contributed the latest medical expertise on each topic so that these stories can best help other patients, families and caregivers understand how children perceive and work through their own challenges.

**Text:** Hey Gee and Grace Bowden
**Illustrations:** Hey Gee

**Medical editor:** Robert M. Jacobson, M.D., Division of Community Pediatric and Adolescent Medicine,
Department of Pediatric and Adolescent Medicine, Children's Center, Mayo Clinic, Rochester, MN

**Managing editor**: Anna Cavallo, Health Education and Content Services/Mayo Clinic Press, Mayo Clinic, Rochester, MN
**Project manager:** Kim Chandler, Department of Education, Mayo Clinic, Rochester, MN
**Manager of publications:** Céline Colombier-Maffre, Fondation Ipsen, Paris, France
**President:** James A. Levine, M.D., Ph.D., Professor, Fondation Ipsen, Paris, France

MAYO CLINIC PRESS
200 First St. SW
Rochester, MN 55905
mcpress.mayoclinic.org

The information in this book is true and complete to the best of our knowledge. This book is intended only as an informative guide for
those wishing to learn more about health issues. It is not intended to replace, countermand or conflict with advice given to you by your
own physician. The ultimate decision concerning your care should be made between you and your doctor. Information in this book is
offered with no guarantees. The author and publisher disclaim all liability in connection with the use of this book.

For bulk sales to employers, member groups and health-related companies, contact Mayo Clinic, 200 First St. SW, Rochester, MN 55905,
or send an email to SpecialSalesMayoBooks@mayo.edu.

**Proceeds from the sale of every book benefit important medical research and education at Mayo Clinic.**

ISBN 978-1-945564-07-9

Library of Congress Control Number: 2021950899

Printed in the United States of America